T0157841

NEWS ABOUT COLORED PEOPLE

NEWS ABOUT COLORED PEOPLE

DORIS LANDRUM

authorHOUSE®

AuthorHouse™
1663 Liberty Drive
Bloomington, IN 47403
www.authorhouse.com
Phone: 1-800-839-8640

Published by AuthorHouse   08/26/2016

ISBN: 978-1-4634-2263-9 (sc)
ISBN: 978-1-4634-2262-2 (e)

Print information available on the last page.

This book is printed on acid-free paper.

This book is dedicated to the loving memories of my parents, Willie and Gurt and to my sisters, Velma and Charlene.
I would also like to recognize my wonderful aunts, uncles, and cousins. They always filled our home with endless laughter whenever they visited.
I have to apologize to my brother Charles Landrum. I completely forgot to include him in the story!
I'd also like to dedicate this book to the 'youngins' of our clan. You never met 'Uncle Buddy' or Papa Sam Reed. You've never used an 'outhouse,' drank water from an actual 'well' or slept on a 'pallet.'
To that I say, "Ask your parents about the old days!"
Family history should be kept alive.

CONTENTS

PROLOGUE

Historians have labeled 1967 as the "Summer of Love". They were referring to the "hippies" of Haight-Ashbury in California. Of course, those flower children were light years away from where we lived in Newport, Arkansas. My 'Summer of Love' in 1967 had nothing to do with the communal living and oddly dressed young people on the west coast.

I'm not certain why this particular time resonates in my memory bank. Surely there is a reason why this year fills every cavity of my brain whenever I find myself reminiscent about the past. But for the life of me I can't pen down any one single reason.

Maybe it was the biblically dressed character that moved onto Clay Street into one of Mrs. Sheila Thornton's rent houses. As you may have guessed, this incident alone caused many speculating tongues to wag.

Then again, it could have been the elaborate wedding held at First Baptist Church just days before the Fourth of July.

This was such a spectacular event that it has served as a benchmark for all other weddings I would attend for years to come.

Still this was a time when the seeds of new friends were planted while the bond between old friends grew even stronger.

Yes, the historic 'Summer of Love' was a memorable time for me.

It was three months filled with fleeting moments of joy, pain and personal growth.

In 1967 my family which was composed of my parents, two sisters, and my brother lived in a small A-framed white house. It was nestled safely and quite conveniently by Mrs. Daisy McDaniel's grocery store on Clay Street in Newport, Arkansas. We had moved there five years earlier when my brother was still a toddler. I remember being excited about the move to Clay Street. The new place had a screened in front porch and plenty of rooms. Our old place on Front Street was a 'shot gun' house with only four rooms.

Newport is just one of the hundreds of small towns that crisscross Arkansas also known as The Natural State. It is located in the northeast and is sandwiched between Little Rock and Memphis, Tennessee. Little Rock is about eighty-six miles to the west and Memphis approximately ninety miles (or more) to the east.

During World War II, Newport was home to over 3500 servicemen who trained at the nearby airbase. It was also about this time that Sam Walton, of Walmart fame, opened his first business here in Newport. It was a five and ten cents store which was located downtown.

Our little hamlet is also home base to several nationally known and celebrated figures. We have a member of the Baseball Hall of Fame, an Academy Award winning actress and a former member of the Pittsburgh Steelers, all having roots here in Newport, Arkansas.

However, our most famous (or infamous) resident is the notorious White River Monster. He's a mythical, dinosaur-type creature supposedly birthed in the White River, the local waterway. Sightings of 'Whitey' date all the way back to the days of the War Between the States. Other than being allegedly responsible for the overturning of boats during the Civil War, the 'monster' has posed no threat to the town residents. Although, every once in a while news will surface of a sighting by a local resident or tourist.

The population of Newport, Arkansas in 1967 hovered somewhere around sixty-five hundred to seven thousand people. The racial make—up placed the Caucasian population in the majority with the African American the minority. . . but not by much.

The racial lines during the latter part of the 1960s were well defined. From Remmel Street on back to Garfield, Clay, Calhoun Circle, Mason and Vine were all primarily 'colored neighborhoods'.

Neighborhoods in and around Newport High and Castleberry Schools were white.

The local schools were still segregated and would remain so until the early 70s.

Segregation was still alive and well in Newport in 1967 but it clearly was on life support. To quote a famous songwriter "The times were a'changin."

Even though, the 'white' and 'colored' signs had been removed from a local (and very popular) eatery downtown. This didn't stop some people from still robotically sitting in their former racially assigned areas.

In spite of these racially divided lines, there was a certain pride and dignity held by the people in our community.

One grand way this pride was displayed was through an important article which ran in the local newspaper.

On a weekly basis The Newport Daily Independent featured a column entitled: News About Colored People. Its purpose was to focus on the positive occurrences both minor and major of the black community.

Newsworthy items such as your child heading off to school or to the armed services and visiting out-of-town guests were important to the readers. Having one's name appear in this column would be the topic of conversation for days to come.

Pride was also shown in our school.

The yearly Christmas Pageants held at WF Branch High School Auditorium were always impressive affairs. There were spectacular performances from the singing angels and readings of the written word on down to the gospel choir.

The other impressive events held at Branch would be the end of the year spring rituals.

It started with the Prom held in April and was followed by the Baccalaureate and Graduation ceremonies in May. All of these activities kept families buzzing with excitement until the end of the year.

These end of the year activities were held in our gymnasium. The Baccalaureate and Graduation ceremonies were real family affairs both immediate and extended. The unofficial community elders (Big Mamas, Ministers, Church Mothers and other Church Folk) attended EVERY Graduation. The young people in our community got plenty of support.

There was pride in our Neighborhoods.

I grew up in a time when we referred to our community as a neighborhood, because that's exactly what it was. Adults praised and encouraged you for your good works and model behavior. They also could and would chastise you when you acted in a way that didn't represent you, your family, or your community in a respectable manner.

This was made possible because there was a well drawn line between adult and child. A line that as a child you didn't dare cross.

Adults were properly addressed as 'Mr. Smith' or 'Mrs. Lane.' The replies of 'yeah or naw' were frowned on as a response to a question posed to you by an adult. And by all that is holy, you never called anyone over the age of twenty-five by their first name (learned that the hard way!)

One of the most important things I remember about growing up in Newport was that we were expected to move past the cotton fields and the kitchens of white people. Achieving this goal might take one of several avenues: College, trade school, or the military.

Another way of achieving this goal would be to travel 'north' to a relative's house. Here you would most likely get a job in one of the local factories. This was especially true for those who moved to areas like Chicago or Detroit.

Whatever road one would take in their post high school journey, the goal was the same: Achievement of the American Dream.

CHAPTER 1

Mr. Chuck And The Horse In The Gray Flannel Suit

Monday, June 26

The most remarkable part of the summer of 1967 had its genesis the last week of June during my mother's vacation.

"Doris Marie, come here. I need you to go to Mrs. Daisy McDaniel's store. We need some cornmeal and buttermilk for supper tonight, and check to see if we have any sugar for the kool-aid."

Mama's voice was loud and clear as it bellowed to the living room from the back porch. I had just settled down a few minutes ago to watch my favorite game show and definitely didn't feel like moving.

"Can it wait a few minutes, Mama? I want to finish watching THE DATING GAME. Why can't Charlene go?"

"I didn't call Charlene... I called you!"

"Two minutes that's all I need mama two minutes!"

"Doris Marie Jimmerson you better get your little square butt in here to get this money for the store! RIGHT NOW LITTLE GIRL!"

It was at this point that I almost left my shadow behind trying to get to the back porch where mama was folding the laundry. You know your parents always mean business when they summon you by your whole name.

My sister Charlene and I had just brought the clothes in from the line about 20 minutes ago. Mama was on the back porch busy folding and sorting all the pants, shirts, sheets, and pillowcases into sections on the makeshift laundry table.

Mama once said that she didn't mind folding laundry because it seemed to relax her. Quite often she could be heard singing while she placed the freshly washed items onto the table. Of course, it would depend on the mood she was in as to what kind of song she'd be singing. Her repertoire was quite extensive. If something was heavy on her mind, she'd probably be singing a church tune or maybe a blues melody (either fits sometime when you're low.)

Frankly, you could never tell with my mother, she might be singing something by The Rolling Stones. Her favorite song was 'Satisfaction.'

By the time I got to the back porch, Mama already had the money waiting for me.

"Now, what did I say we needed?" Being questioned was a standard ritual before being sent off on any errand.

"Eh, you said cornmeal, buttermilk, and sugar." I repeated the list very quickly and quite proudly. I wanted her to be impressed by my powers of recall.

"Little Miss, I believe I said to check to see if we NEEDED any sugar before buying it didn't I?"

"Why yes, you did say that. I believe it was right before you told me to get my little square butt out here."

I belted out those words with a big grin hoping I'd read correctly that slight smile mama seemed to have on her face.

"Oh I got your little square butt!" She laughingly said that while swatting me on the rear.

My mother, Gurtha Lean Jimmerson was in a good mood most of the time and today was no exception. She had an upbeat personality and genuine concern for others. Gurt (as she was known by most people) had a magnetic personality that naturally drew people to her. Most folks found it quite easy to engage her in conversation whenever they met on the street.

If it was someone she'd known for quite a while and was around her age it was "Hey Gurt!" Greetings from young people would always be "Hey, Mrs. Gurtha Lean". After which, mama would spend just the right length of time chatting and getting caught up.

"Now, here is two dollars. This should be enough." Mama carefully placed the money in my hand.

Oh Yeah it was enough alright. As a matter of fact, there might be enough change left over for a 'Baby Ruth' my favorite candy bar.

"And Doris Marie, make sure you bring me back my change."

Mama will say that now, but I guarantee you that if she's busy when I return, she will have forgotten all about that change. Especially if I sneak back into the kitchen while she is busy somewhere else in the house.

"And make sure you come right back. I've got to get supper on the table before your daddy gets home."

Of course, I'd come right back and quickly. I mean, Mrs. McDaniel's store IS right next door to our house. This was also a gathering place for the neighborhood. So once you got there, you were subject to finding a friend or two. You might also get a chance to listen in on some of the grownups' gossip and this could cause you to lose all track of time.

I spotted Mr. Chuck, one of Mrs. McDaniel's regulars, as soon as I came in the store. He was our neighborhood handyman or rather he was THE neighborhood handyman. He could fix just about anything. Mrs. McDaniel quite often used him to help out around the store. He stocked the shelves, repaired the refrigerator, and swept out the store.

You might also find him mowing the lawns and making repairs for her rental properties.

Mr. Chuck spent his evenings watching the news on Mrs. McDaniel's store TV. As Mr. Chuck saw it, he didn't see any need to buy one when he could watch it for free there in the store. He seemed to have two favorite programs: The Evening News with Walter Cronkite and later on. . . Laugh In. Go Figure Mr. Chuck for a Laugh In fan.

In the summer of '67 Mr. Chuck had to be in his mid to late 60s. He wasn't a very tall man, but couldn't be described as short either. If you caught him early enough in the morning, you would see him in his freshly ironed and beautifully creased denim overalls which he wore most every day.

In the fall and winter the ensemble was completed with muted colored flannel shirts. In the spring and summer he'd polish off the set with a white short sleeved tee shirt.

The numerous lines and deep crevices in Mr. Chuck's very dark skin told the story of his life's journeys. He had many stories on how he worked his way off a farm down in Florida and travelled to the bright lights of Harlem in New York. Now just how he wound up in Newport is anybody's guess. Daddy never talked about it and he and Mr. Chuck often spoke.

One of Mr. Chuck's funniest stories involved seeing a man with a face and head of a horse. I don't mean he had horse-like features, but the man actually had the head and face of a horse!

The 'Horse-man's' oversized ears served as bookends for the small tuft of hair situated right in center of his head. The long eyelashes complimented his big horse-like eyes. And of course there was the enormous horse snout and teeth. It was almost as if someone had taken the actual head of a horse and placed it on the body of a man!

Mr. Chuck swears that he first saw this "horse-man" on a street in Little Rock. The Horseman was wearing a gray flannel suit and he carried a briefcase.

Yes, a gray flannel suit with a briefcase. Apparently, Mr. Horseman was a member of the Little Rock business community. Remember Mr. Chuck said that he had a head like a horse. The rest of the Horseman was quite human.

Now here is maybe the oddest part of the story. One day Mr. Chuck made a point of shadowing the Horseman. He wanted to see just how a man who looked like a horse spent his time.

After a day of intense observations, Mr. Chuck concluded that with few exceptions the horseman was pretty normal.

He got his mail at the post office.

He went to his bank to cash a check.

Finally, he did a bit of shopping at a local Kroger's store.

He reportedly bought an unusual amount of apples, 3 large sacks of sugar, and 10 boxes of oatmeal and other dry cereal. Not too strange!

As kids we loved this story and even though it was quite farfetched, we knew not to challenge Mr. Chuck on it.

We grew up in a time when there was an invisible line drawn between the child and the adult. And as a child YOU DIDN'T CROSS THAT LINE! If an adult told you something you pretty much accepted it and moved on, and you kept your doubts to yourself.

Besides, who wouldn't want to believe that somewhere there really was a man who looked like a horse?!

. . . . who wore a gray flannel suit

. . . . and carried a briefcase

. . . . and drove a Mustang (how ironic!)

Cousin Bobby's Chocolate Chip Geyser

I spoke to Mrs. McDaniel and the rest of the adults. After engaging in some harmless trash talking with some of my friends, I finally purchased the items Gurthalean had needed for supper.

And wouldn't you know it? I HAD forgotten to check the cabinet to see if we needed more sugar, so I got some anyway. After all, it is summer and we were destined to drink our weight in Kool-aid and lemon aid. Having a little extra sugar in the cabinet won't hurt a bit.

Finally it's time to tally up the cornmeal, sugar, and Kool-aid.

"That'll be one dollar and seventy cents, Doris Marie"

Fantastic! Gurthalean had given me two dollars so I had thirty cents change coming. In 1967, I could do some real damage with thirty cents.

What to do? What to do? Finally the answer hit me like a bolt of lightning. I could spend fifteen cents and still have fifteen cents change left over for mama.

"Mrs. Daisy, could I have a BABY RUTH and a nickel's worth of chocolate chip cookies?"

Mrs. McDaniel had THE BEST chocolate chip cookies in Jackson County. There were two very good reasons for that. Each cookie was loaded with chips and you got two cookies for a penny! How great was that?! So, for my paltry five cents I had just purchased ten cookies. . . sweet!

But the downside is I'll most likely have to share with my sister Charlene. When you have brothers and sisters, you rarely could have a treat to yourself. . . . .. you most likely would have to share.

I really didn't mind though. Ten cookies is quite a lot, and we'll each have five so I was okay with that.

Besides, I don't want to be like my cousin Bobby, who was without comparison the stingiest kid on God's earth.

He always wanted you to know when he had something new, but he never wanted to share. If he had some junk food, he would either give you just a very tiny portion or none at all, while making you watch him eat his share!

This brings me to one of my most favorite stories about my cousin Bobby.

Once he purchased twenty cents worth of chocolate chip cookies at the store. This of course meant he had forty cookies and none of which did he share with anyone.

After leaving the store, Bobby rode his bike all through the neighborhood. He finally stopped by our house and was still munching on the cookies. A bunch of us kids were hanging out under the big shade tree that is centered between our house and Mrs. Baxter, our next door neighbor.

Bobby pulls up and immediately starts to brag about his windfall of chocolate chip cookies. And even though I knew he was happy about his mouthwatering treats, I could sense that something was wrong. Bobby was starting to look a bit squeamish.

Did I mention that this story takes place on a particularly hot day in August?

So, after a few nauseous but deliciously munch filled moments, Bobby started a silent countdown of the remaining treats. Everyone in the group quieted down as if we all sensed something big was about to happen.

He was down to five cookies (munch, munch) and four to go.

Four cookies and three to go (munch, munch). . . three cookies and two to go,(munch, munch) two cookies and one to go,(munch, munch).

Now, for the last cookie(munch. . . . .munch.) Finally, that last cookie was eaten and Bobby looked very proud for just about a hot second and then. . . . .. Well, let's just say that Old Faithful of Yellow Stone had some stiff competition that day.

Bobby spewed cookie vomit everywhere! He really did look a little like that geyser from Yellow Stone, only that wasn't warm spring water shooting up from his stomach. He up chucked every cookie he had that day and a few from last week too!

No, James Brown is not Our Cousin!

Now, that I have my items, it's time to make my way home. Thank God my shirt has plenty of room and my savory goodies can be safely hidden away from Gurt's curious gaze.

James Brown's "Try Me" was beaming from WDIA on the radio from the back of Mrs. McDaniel's store. WDIA was a black owned station out of Memphis. Everybody listened to 'DIA. This was the place that played all the latest hits out of Motown and of course, it was the home of the Memphis Sound.

Plus 'DIA had one of the best disc jockeys ever. He was a DJ by the name of Chris the Burner Turner. Sometimes when Chris had a hot record going, he would utter the following words:

"So nice, I'm gonna sock it to you twice!"

Then he would proceed to play the same hot record all over again. How cool is that?!

It was a safe bet that when I did arrive home "Try Me" would probably still be playing. We had a radio strategically placed in the far right corner of our living room.

Daddy liked to brag that this radio was the first brand new piece of furniture that he'd bought after he and mama married in 1947. It was a rather large console radio with a top that opened to reveal the dial and the turntable. Even though I thought it was kind of old fashion, it had one very cool feature. The dial showing the station numbers had a light that grew ever brighter as the day gave way to evening. We didn't use it to spin records very much anymore. My oldest sister, Velma, had recently purchased a portable record player with the money from her job at the hospital.

These days the only time we used the big radio to play records was when Daddy dragged out his old 33 1/3 records at Christmas. His favorite was "Merry Christmas, Baby". Boy did we hate that song.

Finally after a few short steps, I arrive back in our yard. And as luck would have it. . . . no Gurthalean on the front porch. I really was lucky to find the porch empty. Mama's good friend Mrs. Louise hadn't made it down yet. She usually showed up most afternoons to sit and pass the time with mama laughing and talking on our front porch.

Great! No one is on the front porch so I can safely hide my goodies in daddy's toolbox. The green box containing daddy's work tools had an invisible neon sign just above it which read OFF LIMITS TO ALL.

As I approached the unlocked fortress of home repair treasures, I very carefully (and quietly) opened the container and placed my treats right there on top for easy access. All the while I was thinking of how good it was going to taste later on this evening while watching THAT GIRL.

Entering the living room I could see that Charlene had vacated and was most likely off on her bicycle for Remmel Avenue. She'd probably headed over to Michelle, her best friend since first grade.

After making my way to the kitchen to put away the food, I hear Gurthalean calling for me from her bedroom.

I quickly get the fifteen cents change ready for her as I am sure that this will be the first question out of mouth.

"Where's my change little girl?"

And Once again she didn't disappoint. When I get there, I notice that she is reading The Newport Daily Independent, our local newspaper. Gurt was seated on the 'gossip bench' thoroughly mulling over each and every paragraph of every page. To my mother, ALL the news was important. She never relinquished the paper until she had read it from cover to cover.

Gurt generally started off by reading an article written by Mrs. March, one of our local teachers who titled her article: NEWS ABOUT COLORED PEOPLE. This was written to keep us abreast of all the news which affected the black community. The marriages, births, deaths, school graduations, and visiting relatives were all featured in the article.

At the time I didn't care for the title because I thought it made black people sound as though we were from another planet. In retrospect, I realize how important those articles were to our community. We lived in a country that didn't always respect us as citizens. In its own small way Mrs. March's column said that we did indeed matter.

"Guess who is in Mrs. March's column?" Gurthalean belted this info out as soon as I appeared in her doorway. I'm glad she was excited about the article, because she was completely distracted when I handed her the change.

"Don't tell me," I answered, "let me guess. . . . uh, I know. James Brown is coming to town!"

"I know you're kidding," Mama replied, "but it could happen you know he's our cousin."

My mother was born in Macon, Georgia and her maiden name is Brown. Apparently she has a distant cousin who is a cousin to THE James Brown. This is our link to James Brown. But daddy says that this was highly unlikely, especially since the state of Georgia had about a million people with the last name of Brown.

"Ok Mama, if you say so, James Brown IS our cousin.

So what's in NEWS ABOUT 'THE' COLORED PEOPLE?"

"Mrs. March has featured all the kids headed to AM&N this fall and look here is your sister's name."

Gurthalean quickly handed me the newspaper. There it was Velma Jean Jimmerson daughter of Willie and Gurthalean Jimmerson will be a part of the freshman class for 1967-68 at AM&N College in Pine Bluff, Arkansas. Mama was beaming from ear to ear. She was so proud of Velma.

Not only did Mrs. March have the good news about Velma written, she also had her best friend, Laura Marks featured in the article. Both were headed for AM&N in September. This wasn't surprising since the two had been practically joined at the hip since the first grade.

After reading the paper, mama quickly retreated to the kitchen. She was finishing up supper by cooking the cornbread and making the Kool-aid.

As it was her normal practice, Gurthalean had already started to boil the salt meat for the turnip greens and had fried the chicken earlier in the day. As luck would have it, mama was going to bake her famous peach cobbler. Yea! This was a treat that we usually didn't get until Sunday. Because mama was on vacation this week, she had more time around the house. A great benefit of that was a delicious peach cobbler and on a Monday!

It was still early in the afternoon, so I asked mama if I could ride my bike over to my best friend's house. She agreed as long as I was back home by four. Daddy got home by four and we had to be home before him so that we could have supper around four-thirty.

Adventures With Lillian

This was turning out to be a perfect day to ride my bike throughout the neighborhood. Quite often somewhat mild temperatures may still abound in Arkansas during the early part of June. This can give local residents a false sense of what the rest of the summer might have in store for them. But this was the first official week of summer.

Even though the temperatures were slowly creeping up, we had yet to experience the blistering heat that surely awaited us.

Today was particularly beautiful. It was a little cool earlier this morning and the sky had been filled with grayish white clouds. You know the kind of clouds that might suggest rain. But by this afternoon, the clouds had given way to a beautiful blue sky. There was still a cool, crisp feeling in the air making the blue jeans I was wearing very comfortable.

I was headed over to Lillian Jarrett, my best friend. Lillian and her family moved here from Montgomery, Alabama when we were both in fifth grade.

Because her last name started with "Ja" (mine was "Ji") she sat in front of me in all of our classes. Her dad, Mr. David 'Lucky' Jarrett, opened up a barbershop and taxi-stand on Front Street. Her mom, Mrs. Rita Jarrett became the new principal at WF Branch, the local black school.

Lillian was an only child and hanging out at her house was a tremendous amount of fun. There were always lots of snacks in the kitchen and the Jarretts had their TV in an actual den. Most people I knew had a TV either in their living room or in someone's bedroom. The Jarretts had a room that was used specifically for entertainment. I was certain that they were millionaires. And best of all, they had color TV. This was a luxury that most working class people in the 1960's couldn't afford.

I liked color TV. By 1967 a number of programs had gone to color. This made a lot of sense for shows like Bonanza and The Wonderful World of Disney, but not so much for others like The Andy Griffin Show. For me, seeing Andy's court house and Aunt Bee's kitchen in color caused Mayberry to lose all of its small town appeal.

In some ways Lillian and I were complete opposites. She was tall and lanky and had what we used to refer to as "good hair." I on the other hand was a bit shorter and "stouter" with full lips and African kinky, hair. Lillian was very out-going and made friends very easily. I wasn't quite as out-going, but I was friendly once I got to know a person.

Lillian could have been described as stunningly beautiful even at thirteen and I was… well let's just say that most boys weren't rushing to sit beside me during a school assembly. But with all of her family's assets and visible beauty Lillian was one of the most unspoiled kids I'd ever met.

One major way in which Lillian and I were alike was our love for The Beatles (especially Paul) and the whole British Invasion movement. We listened to the latest British hits on station WMPS out of Memphis.

Truth be told, our love for the British wasn't our only reason for listening to WMPS, we also tuned in to hear other American rock groups. In 1967 it wasn't politically correct to be black and readily admit that you liked a white group. Lillian didn't care, she even had pictures of the Beatles, The Rolling Stones and The Young Rascals taped to her bedroom wall. The Rascals weren't British but they were rock n' roll and one of our favorites. Because of their "blue-eye" soulful sound they were one of a very few white groups you might hear on 'DIA on a regular basis.

On the other hand, not only did WMPS play the latest music by popular white artists of the day, they also played the hits out of Motown and Memphis. That's why I kept our radio in the kitchen tuned to WMPS. This way I could listen to all the Top Forty hits while I was washing dishes or working on my homework.

When I finally get to Lillian's yard I noticed her neighbor, Mrs. Joann Weston, standing in her front yard talking to some people from out of town. It was her new son-in-law, Gary and daughter Brenda Ann, who lived in Detroit.

Having been widowed at age thirty-nine, Mrs. Weston raised five children on her own. For a few years she worked as a maid for some lawyer-family in town. This didn't last for too long as Mrs. Weston was far too feisty to sit in someone's backseat or have anyone under the age of thirty call her by her first name. It wasn't long after leaving her housekeeper's job that she would soon find a job as a nurse's aide at GPW Nursing Home. Besides, Mrs. Weston had three older sons: Darrell, Bradley, and Terrance Weston who all kept jobs to help out around the house.

Her oldest daughter, Loretta also worked. She and my sister Velma worked in the kitchen at Newport Hospital. Brenda Ann who was nicknamed 'Doll' never worked outside of her mother's house. But it was her job to help keep everything neat and tidy at home.

This wasn't a job that Doll took lightly as this was also the way in which she earned her allowance. Being the youngest, Doll was a bit spoiled. It wasn't in a bratty sort of way, but more in a sheltered way. She wasn't allowed to 'keep company' or date boys until she was a junior in high school.

But it wasn't until she went away to college that she would find true love. His name was Gary Riley and they met during their sophomore year at AM&N and married soon after graduation.

Doll and Gary moved to Detroit where he worked on the line at Ford Motor Company. He took college classes at night to get his master's in education. Doll was teaching fifth grade and also taking classes to get her masters in counseling.

This was their first trip home in over a year and I could tell that Mrs. Weston was too happy for words having them here.

"Hey, Mrs. Joann! Hey Doll!" I screamed to the group as I rolled my bike onto Lillian's sidewalk.

"Hey, Doris Marie" Both Mrs. Joann and Doll spoke in unison to return my greeting.

I could hear Doll commenting to Mrs. Joann on how she barely recognized me because I'd grown so much.

I didn't try to engage them in any conversation because I could see that they were trying to get caught up. Besides, I don't think that Mrs. Weston was ready to share Doll with anyone just yet.

I could only imagine the huge feast that was about to greet the young couple in the Weston home.

As soon as I get to Lillian's front porch, I notice the door is slightly ajar and she is peeking out and motioning for me to quickly come in. It wasn't like Lillian to be so mysterious. My curiosity was definitely peaked and I had to find out what was about to happen.

"Doris Marie, come here quick!" Lillian loudly whispered as she pulled me inside.

"Who are those people in Mrs. Joann's yard?" Lillian immediately began to quiz me about the unusual events unfolding next door.

"That's Mrs. Joann's daughter, Doll and her husband Gary. They live in Detroit." I know that Lillian's family had only lived here for a few years, but how could she not know Doll? Had she never talked to Mrs. Joann?

"Haven't you ever been over to Mrs. Joann's house? She's got like a million pictures of all of her kids."

Lillian said she had been over to Mrs. Joann's but she didn't recall or had forgotten any picture she'd seen of Doll. Besides, Lillian assured me that she would indeed remember seeing any photo of Gary.

So it appears that someone has a little crush on their neighbor. Crushes on boys were hardly a new phenomenon. We both had a crush on Paul McCartney, Marvin Gaye, Smokey Robinson and on Felix Cavaliere from the Rascals. But those were safe crushes because it wasn't like we were ever going to meet any of those people.

Lillian had other real life crushes on boys at school. But none of her school crushes or her "music world" crushes seem to compare to this. Lillian was the most outgoing person I knew. But now she had been reduced to hiding in her house, terrified of meeting the handsome stranger next door!

"Let's go ride our bikes over to Calhoun Circle" I was anxious to get some free time in before having to go back home for supper.

"I'm not going out there!" Lillian was actually in a panic at the thought of seeing Gary up close.

"Then let's go watch TV. WHERE THE ACTION IS is probably on now let's go watch it."

Lillian consented and we went down into the den where the big TV was to watch it in color. Paul Revere and the Raiders were always on Where The Action is. Today Martha Reeves and The Vandellas were also going to be on the program. Both groups were favorites of ours.

As always the show was great fun to watch. The Vandellas did one of their old hits "Nowhere to Run" and the Raiders did their recent hit "Good Thing". The show was filled with the usual fun-filled antics of the Raiders along with some great music.

Finally, Lillian got her courage together to go outside with me to ride our bikes. It's around three fifteen and I have less than an hour of free time before going home for supper.

"Let's go to the playground" I knew if we headed first to the playground in Calhoun Circle there would be a good chance we'd see some of our friends.

We head out from Lillian's house on Mason Street. Fortunately Mrs. Joann and her family had gone inside saving Lillian the embarrassment of wetting her pants from the sheer excitement of meeting Gary!

We then make our way onto Clay Street to quickly stop at my house and check in with mama.

We ride our bikes around to the back of the house then pop upon the back porch. After entering the kitchen, we can smell the aroma of mama's planned evening meal. Mama and her friend, Mrs. Louise are seated at the table enjoying a cold glass of ice tea.

"Hi, Mrs. Louise." "Hi Mrs. Gurthalean." Lillian beat me speaking to everyone.

"Hi, Mrs. Louise."

Mrs. Louise Taylor was about ten years older than my mother and they had been friends for many years. I was surprised to see them in the kitchen. Mrs. Louise's favorite pastime was sitting with mama on our front porch. It was the perfect vantage point to watch some of the comings and goings often associated with Mrs. Daisy McDaniels' store.

"Hi, girls. Lillian, how are your parents doing?" Mrs. Louise was the first to address the two of us. You always felt that she was genuinely glad to see you whenever she spoke.

"They're okay, Mrs. Louise. Mama said you had on another pretty hat at church last Sunday"

"It was alright, but it didn't compare to the hats your mother sports every Sunday." Mrs. Louise was right. Even though she could wear some outstanding hats (one which has what I believe to be ostrich feathers) Lillian's mother could "out-hat" her.

"Well, Miss Doris Marie I guess you are very proud of your sister." Mrs. Louise was poking around to see if I had something good to say about Velma.

"I can't wait for her to leave. She's always trying to boss people around." I was just voicing the eternal fake complaint of every younger sister.

"Louise, don't pay that girl any attention. She knows she is going to miss her big sister when she leaves for school." By this time mama had walked over to give Lillian a hug.

"Well, I guess I'll miss her a little bit." Mama gave me a light thump on the nose for that remark.

"Mama, is it okay if I ride my bike to the playground with Lillian?"

This question was mostly just a formality. Mama never minded my riding around the neighborhood with Lillian. Lillian was an even-tempered kid, who never got into trouble. . . . plus she came from what Gurt deemed to be a 'very good family.' Mama said that it was okay as long I was home before Daddy got off work.

Zach, Dexter, and Lynn

Lillian and I got on our bikes and started out for the playground. It wasn't until we got to the end of Clay Street that I realized that I had forgotten my "goodies" from my earlier trip to Mrs. McDaniels's store.

But no matter, Lillian had some money and she didn't mind sharing. . . . within reason of course.

As luck would have it, we soon came up on Sloan Grocery Store. Mr. Sloan's store was situated in a pretty lucrative place on Remmel Avenue. This area might be described as the dividing line between the Black and White neighborhoods. Mr. Sloan got trade from both areas.

Mr. Sloan was a tall and very stout man who reminded me of Dan Blocker who played "Hoss" on BONANZA.

If you didn't know any better, you'd think he was the meanest person on God's Earth. The reality was that Mr. Sloan was quite a congenial man, who treated everyone with respect.

His son, Zachery, was equally agreeable and quite handsome. Zachery was about fourteen and wore his hair like Paul McCartney. Sometimes when he gave you change, he would even toss his hair like Paul.

Zachery usually only worked in the store two days a week. He'd work Monday and Tuesday one week then Thursday and Friday the next week. There was the rare occasion when he'd work on a Wednesday.

Lillian and I concluded that working in his father's store was probably how Zachery earned his allowance.

Most days when you entered the store, you would find Zachery perched atop a stool behind the counter. He'd have his radio tuned to WMPS while he thumbed through some magazine.

When Lillian and I got there today, we found Zachery sitting on his stool reading Hit Parade magazine. Van Morrison's song, 'Brown Eyed Girl' was coming to an end on the radio.

"May I help you?" Zachery put down the magazine and dismounted his stool to assist us.

Mr. Sloan's store was well stocked. However, unlike Mrs. McDaniel's store his establishment wasn't quite as cluttered with merchandise.

He may have had more space in his store but he didn't have Mrs. McDaniel's famous two for a penny chocolate chip cookies!

After looking into the candy case, I decided on a pack of Lemon Heads and Lillian got the same. By this time "Penny Lane" by the Beatles is playing on the radio and Lillian and I start to sing along. We weren't immediately aware of the fact that Zachery was also singing.

After another moment, everyone looked at each other and laughed at our attempts to sing like the "Fab Four".

"Y'all like the Beatles too?" Zach stopped laughing long enough to ask a rather curious question.

'Did WE like the Beatles?' At first the "mini black militant" part of me was a bit offended. I mean, why wouldn't we like The Beatles? The first time they were on Ed Sullivan the streets were practically emptied of teenagers EVERYWHERE. So, why wouldn't we like them too?

I guess I would be equally inquisitive if I learned that Zachery was a fan of someone like James Brown. But, who am I kidding? Everybody likes James Brown!

"Yeah, we love John, Paul, George, and Ringo. My friend here has the new album." I proudly pointed my thumb in Lillian's direction who seemed a bit irritated with the notion of being singled out.

Zachery asked Lillian about her favorite song on the album. He was surprised when he learned that she liked 'Yellow Submarine' which was also one of his favorites.

After sharing a brief moment on our mutual admiration for the Fab Four, Lillian led a rather quick retreat from Mr. Sloan's Store. I hastily followed suit. She still seemed a bit irritated when we mounted our bikes to complete our journey to the playground.

"You mad at me Lillian?" I had to ask because it seemed all too obvious that she was 'out of sorts' about something.

"No, I'm not mad at you, Doris Marie. I'm just a bit irritated."

"With me?" Now I'm wondering just what I had done to cause this bad feeling in Lillian.

"No, it just bothers me when white people act like all black people are the same. Just because we're black we aren't suppose to even know who the Beatles are let alone like their music."

I forgot that Lillian, who was one of the most even tempered persons I knew, still carried the scars of being raised in Montgomery, Alabama. Her parents had even taken part in the Bus Boycott in 1955.

"Zachery probably thinks that we only listen to the blues on WDIA."

Man she really was irritated if she's talking about us listening to the blues. Everybody knows that only old people listen to the Blues.

"Aw, leave Zachery alone. Besides, I think he's kind of cute."

As soon as I said it, I wanted to grab every letter of every word and stuff them back in my mouth.

"You think some white boy is cute? Doris Marie you got to be kidding me." Lillian almost wrecked her bicycle asking me that question.

"Well, you think Paul McCartney is cute!" I took a lot of joy in reminding her of that fact.

"We BOTH think Paul McCartney is cute! Besides, that's different... He's English. Everyone knows that English white people are more cultured and sophisticated than American white people." Lillian delivered this line with the greatest of confidence.

"Girl, that is so stupid. Who told you that?" I almost regretted asking the question after seeing the determined look on Lillian's face.

"Look at the facts. The English have Queen Elizabeth and the royal family and they live in a palace. LBJ is a cowboy that lives on a ranch with a bunch of stinking cows!"

With that we both started to laugh thus ending the heated discussion. This is another reason why we were such good friends. Neither of us liked confrontation. We thought it was time consuming and a waste of energy. Our time was winding down and we weren't going to spend it discussing American white people versus English white people.

When we arrived, the playground was filled with people.

Calhoun Circle's playground had unofficial sectioned areas for each group.

From early morning to mid afternoon, the swings, merry-go-round, and monkey bars were strictly for the little ones and the pre-teens. This changed in the late, late afternoons and evenings when the same equipment was used by the older teenagers for 'courting' purposes.

The playground was more of a meeting place for the teenagers. You wouldn't find a large number of the older kids on the playground during the day. Mainly because any number of the older teens were most likely working on some government sponsored summer project or on some other job around town.

After quickly scanning the area, we find a few of our friends including my sister, Charlene. She and her friend Michelle were gathered beneath one of only three trees on the play ground.We decided to ride our bikes over for a few minutes.

"Does Mama know that you're over here?" Charlene took a few seconds from ruining yet another Supreme's song by 'loud talking' me in front of her friends.

"Yeah, and for your information I just left home and mama said it was okay as long as I got back there before daddy."

I was especially surprised to see her friend Michelle on the playground. Here was a person who never liked to get her clothes the least bit dirty. If her sneakers got dusty or a hint of grass stains, it would upset her for days. I was wondering just what Charlene said to get Michelle to come to the playground today and then I spotted my answer. . . Dexter White.

Dexter White was probably the cutest boy at WF Branch High School. He had hazel-colored eyes with dark brown skin. His hair was brownish black and shaped in a low afro.

Dexter would be starting his junior year this fall. He didn't have a steady girlfriend, although he was chased by many, none stuck so far. I think part of that is because in addition to being the cutest boy at Branch, Dexter was also the smartest and busiest. He was president of his tenth grade class and had been on honor roll since elementary school. He was also on the basketball team as well as the debate team and in the gospel choir.

This fall, Dexter will be one of several students scheduled to take Latin and Trigonometry at Newport High. These were classes that weren't offered at Branch but might be needed to complete some college applications. This would be a new adventure for both schools. We were all interested to see just how it would turn out.

Dexter and his best friend, Lynn Smalls, were handing out fliers about the upcoming 4th of July Extravaganza. This was an annual event sponsored by the local churches. It started with fireworks at Jacksonport State Park and ended with a "social" (dance) at Branch gym.

The "4th" was such a major event in our neighborhood that people planned their family reunions around it. Barbeques pits were set up in just about every back yard in town. Kids donned their new outfits and proudly displayed them while riding their bikes up and down the streets. Packs of teenage girls with freshly pressed hair roamed the streets for hours to nowhere in particular. Mostly they were walking just to be seen.

This is the time of the year when the streets of our little hamlet would be filled with scores of unfamiliar vehicles. The most popular places to find these cars would be at Ted's Lunchroom, the local diner, or at Mr. Jarrett's Barber shop. There you'd find out —of—town license plates attached to some very attractive cars.

Personally, I had mixed feelings about the "4th". Once I learned in Social Studies class that it was the colonists' freedom from British rule and black people were still enslaved, I wondered why we were celebrating.

Of course those questionable thoughts were soon tossed aside when I remembered the new shorts set and sneakers mama would buy for me for the holiday.

The Fourth of July was one of four days of the year in which you were guaranteed a new outfit (the other days being Easter, the first day of school, and Christmas.)

After spending about fifteen minutes circling the playground, Lynn and Dexter both found their way to the place where Charlene and our friends were assembled.

"Hey, Dexter! Hey Lynn!" *Charlene and her friends quickly greeted the two while looking very proud that the popular twosome had joined them under the shade tree.*

"Hello ladies! Don't forget the 4th of July Extravaganza. I know you're going to be there, Doris Marie." *Dexter pulled me away from the others and we waltzed around the group.*

I know Dexter was just teasing me, but did he really have to ask? I mean, in addition to his undeniable cuteness was his unmistakable charisma. If he set up camp on Jupiter, I'd be on the next space flight out just to accompany him (this could only happen after I poisoned all the other girls at school! Yes, he was THAT CUTE!)

"How about you Miss Skinny legs and all, are you gonna be there?!" *Lynn had sneaked up behind Lillian and lightly thumped her ear.*

"Stop talking to me Lynn with your big-head self!" *You could tell that Lillian was only mildly annoyed with Lynn. She had that glimmer of a smile that people get when they are trying to conceal their laughter.*

Lynn Smalls was a tall lanky teenager who had only recently grown into his rather large ears. He was Lillian's first cousin and since she was an only child, he took it upon himself to play the role of her irritating big brother. He was very good at his job and teased Lillian mercilessly every chance he got.

"Who are you taking to the social, Dexter?" *My sister could be so fast sometimes. But she did ask a question that was on everyone's mind.*

"I'm not sure, but I think he's taking his cousin, Belinda Thompson 'Big Belinda." *By this time, Lynn had completely taken over Lillian's bike and was sitting on it much to her protests. He quickly offered up this information with an unusually large smile on his face.*

"That's only because your mama turned me down last minute!" *Dexter didn't even stop waltzing me around to respond to Lynn's teasing. He couldn't let Lynn upstage him. . . . especially in front of his adoring fans.*

Fortunately both Lynn and Dexter were such good friends that they could joke with each other like that.

In our neighborhood, playing the dozens with the wrong two people could easily start a colossal fight.

After a few more minutes of pleasant exchanges, the boys exited our little corner to canvas the rest of the playground. If the 4th of July activities were not successful, it certainly wouldn't be through lack of effort on their part.

Meet Sheritha, Our Best Friend

It was getting late and we didn't see our friend, Sheritha anywhere on the playground. Lillian and I decided to ride over to her apartment there in Calhoun Circle.

Sheritha Evans was a tall and ever growing twelve year old girl. Unlike her thick hair and dark skin which she hadn't quite yet embraced, her height was the one physical feature which she loved. Personally, I thought that her dark skin and thick mane was beautiful. She reminded me of a young Gloria Foster, one of my favorite actresses.

Sheritha used to live down the street from my family. She and her mom, Carmen Evans, moved to Calhoun Circle several years after the project apartments went up in 1962.

They had been living in one of Mrs. McDaniel's many rent houses on Clay Street. Most of the houses were in pretty good shape, but Mrs. Carmen's family had the misfortune to live in the only "shot-gun" house on the block. It was somewhat run down, but Sheritha's mom kept it looking very nice both inside and out. She (like the other ladies on the block), kept a flower bed filled with elephant ears and other colorful flowers. Sheritha said that her mom wanted to move to Calhoun Circle because the apartments were newer and bigger than their house.

"Well, hello Lillian and Doris Marie what are you girls up to this afternoon?" Sheritha's grandmother, Mother Ann, was outside watering the elephant ears and azaleas as she did every afternoon.

"How are you doing, Mother Ann? We just came by to see if Sheritha can ride bikes with us for a while." Lillian answered for the both of us.

"I guess I do very well for an ol' lady and thank you for asking.

How your folks doing, Doris Marie? I read in the COLORED PEOPLE's article that your big sister and Laura Marks are headed to AM&N this fall."

"Everybody's fine at my house, Mother Ann. Mama and daddy are real excited about Velma going to school except daddy doesn't want her to leave Arkansas when she graduates."

"Oh, you tell Butterbean to let that girl alone. These young people don't want to stay around here.

How are your folks doin' Lillian?"

"They're OK, Mother Ann. My mama is gonna have to come by here and get some of your pretty flowers."

"Tell her to come on by. I'd be glad to set her up with some of my prize Azaleas and roses. Y'all like green tomatoes? I got some planted around back."

"Yes ma'am, my daddy loves fried green tomatoes. We eat them all the time! I'll tell Mama what you said"

Lillian loved talking to Mother Ann. Her grandparents still lived in Alabama and she didn't get a chance to see them very often. She really missed seeing her grandmother which is why she loved it when we visited with Sheritha. Mother Ann gave off warm 'grandmotherly' feelings.

We were just about to knock on the door when Sheritha appeared and ushered us inside. Miss Carmen and her Aunt Theola were in the kitchen cooking. Something smelled really good.

"Hi, girls come on in and sit down. Your buddy Sheritha can't go anywhere for the rest of the day. Want to tell them why, Sheritha?" Miss Carmen was pleasant enough, but it looks like Sheritha's mouth had gotten her into some trouble.....again.

"What did you do, Sheritha?" Lillian who never gets into trouble with her mother was a little too eager to find out about Sheritha's offense.

"She's just mad because I left two pans in the sink to soak overnight. If she didn't get up at the crack of dawn she wouldn't found out! Sheritha whispered the last part. She didn't want to make her mother angrier than she already was.

"Mama, can I please, please, please go ride bikes with my friends?" Sheritha was desperate to get outside so, she made sure she used her most pleading voice.

"No ma'am, you CAN NOT please, please, please go ride bikes with your friends. Sheritha, you know better than to ask me to do something when I've said no."

I could tell that Mrs. Carmen wasn't that angry, but she needed (as parents often do) to let Sheritha know that she meant business.

"Sheritha, you can still visit with your friends in your room or y'all can go outside and visit with Granny."

"C'mon y'all let's go to my room." Sheritha and her mom lived in this apartment and Mother Ann (Mrs. Carmen's mother) and her sister Theola lived next door. Most evenings they had supper at Mother Ann's apartment, but today supper was at Mrs. Carmen. I think it was because Mother Ann and Aunt Theola were having Mission Meeting in their apartment.

We followed Sheritha to her room, but reminded her that we couldn't stay long because it was close to suppertime. Sheritha's radio was tuned to WDIA and "All I Need" by the Temptations was playing.

We loved that song.

'all. . . all I need, is just to hear you say, you forgive me. . . . forgive me, baby.'

Of the three of us, Sheritha had the best voice and Lillian had the worst. Maybe it wasn't so bad, but just not quite as good as me and Sheritha. Lillian didn't have a very 'soulful' voice. She faired better when we sang songs by the Monkees or The Lovin' Spoonful.

"Sheritha, you think your mama will let you go to the Free Show on Friday Morning? They're showing "Jason and Argonauts." I think Lillian may have asked that question because she wanted everyone to stop singing.

"I can go. That is if I stay out of trouble." Sheritha was pretty confident.

"And you will stay out of trouble. . . won't you?!" Lillian sounded funny when she was trying to be bossy.

"Yea, I'll be good, besides my daddy sent me some money for a new Fourth of July outfit. Mama will probably let me have some of it for the movies."

"Great! So it's settled. . . we are all going to the Free Show on Friday. Lillian sounded as though she was getting ready to take us on a long road trip.

"Hey, Sheritha guess who we just saw on the playground?" I hope she didn't think I was rubbing her punishment in her face by mentioning a place that was off limits to her.

"Oh, God Doris Marie I hate when you want me to guess something. I never get it right. Why don't you just tell me?" Sheritha could get irritated easily. Today's annoyance was most likely a direct result of her punishment.

"C'mon Sheritha, guess. Who knows you might even get it right." Okay, now I was starting to irritate myself a little.

"If I guess once will you let it go already? Okay, okay, I think Mr. Long was on the playground. Am I right?"

"You wish!" Mr. Long was our Science teacher who bore an uncanny resemblance to Smokey Robinson jade eyes and all.

"No, it wasn't Mr. Long. . . ..we wish it was Mr. Long!" Of the three of us, Lillian had the biggest crush on our very handsome Smokey Robinson type teacher. She took advantage of each and every chance she could get to talk about him.

I finally told her that Dexter and Lynn were there. But of course she was only interested in Dexter. I made sure to let her know that Dexter had danced with me and kissed me on my cheek.

Okay, I made up the kissing part, but I was hoping that Lillian wouldn't rat me out.

Now that I had sufficiently impressed Sheritha, I reminded Lillian that I had to get home. We hastily said our goodbyes to Sheritha and her folks and started on our way.

While riding past the playground, we noticed that it had emptied out of all the little kids and most kids our age. We had just about made it past the area when we spotted Emma Jean Hines and her bunch of thuggish friends. Every neighborhood has their share of bullies and we had Emma Jean and her crowd.

Emma Jean Hines and her cohorts, Verna Dean Jones and Felicia Gail Rucker were always acting as though they owned the neighborhood. On the playground they were known to make people get off the swings or the merry-go-round just so they could have a turn.

And if that wasn't enough, they would monopolize the equipment by staying on as long as they chose. They treated the playground as though it was their own personal property!

As it is with most bullies, this only worked if that person was smaller and /or weaker than they were. These were people who they viewed as being too wimpy to defend themselves. Emma Jean and her girls stalked these 'weaklings' out much like a lion would seek out his prey.

Emma and her bunch were a year older than us. And I must admit that when I was younger I was afraid of them, but now they just look silly. They didn't like Lillian because they said that she thought that she was "white". In their small world, a person who speaks well and is well-mannered is considered white. How dumb is that? Mostly they were jealous of Lillian's long hair and light skin. They always accused her of thinking she was better than anybody else which couldn't be farther from the truth. Lillian was one of the most warmhearted and considerate people I knew.

Fortunately, it appeared that Emma Jean and her band of nasty knuckleheads were busy playing on the merry-go-round. I doubt that they would be their long. The older kids would soon descend onto the playground in another hour or two. When that happens, Emma's bunch will have to relinquish the equipment or they will get a taste of their own medicine.

We took the long way home because I agreed to escort Lillian back to her house. We turned down Garfield from Remmel Avenue and hoped that we wouldn't run into King, the most ferocious German Shepherd in the neighborhood. Even though Lillian and I were deep in conversation, we continued to scan our surroundings for King's familiar growl. We didn't see or hear him and secretly thanked God for our good fortune.

We get to Lillian's house and as luck would have it, there was Doll and her new husband, Gary. They were sitting in the 2-seater, cobalt blue, slide swing on Mrs. Joann's front porch. I'm sure I saw Lillian's face light up as soon as she saw them and by them I mean Gary.

"Hello, Girls." Both Doll and Gary greeted us.

"Hi Doll and uh. . . . Doll's husband" I knew his name but just felt a little strange saying it until we were formally introduced. Poor Lillian hardly said anything at all.

At this time the couple emerge from the slider swing and approach us for a brief conversation.

"Doris Marie, this is my husband Gary Riley."

I don't think that I have ever had an occasion where one adult felt the need to introduce me to another adult. I liked it. It made me feel grown up.

"Hello, Gary. And this is my friend, Lillian Jarrett." Lillian smiles and gives an awkward wave "hello" with her right hand. Doll and her husband both smile and wave back in a similar fashion.

Doll gives Gary a quick history of my family and her relationship with us. She then begins to make her acquaintance with Lillian. This made Lillian feel so much more at ease and she began to talk more and by more, I mean to Gary.

"Lillian, could I borrow your bike for a moment?" Gary was taking advantage of Lillian's obvious 'school girl crush' on him. Although a bit startled by his request, she couldn't say 'yes' fast enough.

Gary corraled the bicycle and rode down Garfield Street. He stopped just short of Remmel Avenue before turning around and riding back.

"Gary's just like a big kid. Don't be surprised if you see him out here one day trying to jump rope with you guys!"

Well Doll just put an idea in Lillian's head. It happens that she has a jump rope. We haven't used it lately, but something tells me it will be coming out of hiding very soon.

"Here you go Miss Lillian Jarrett and thanks for the ride." Gary hands the bike over to Lillian and then kissed her on the cheek. And before either of us could quite interpret what had just happened, he then kissed me on the cheek.

"Gary, you need to stop teasing these girls!" Doll pulled him back to Mrs. Joann's house.

"I was just playing with them. They know it don't you girls?" Gary knew he had two giggly preteens who he could easily impress with just a wink of those brown eyes!

"We don't mind, Miss Doll" Lillian was so flustered she called Doll "Miss".

"Naw, we don't mind. We knew he was just playing with us." I was a bit flustered myself.

"I have got to get home before my daddy gets there." In all the excitement I very nearly forgot about supper.

"Bye, y'all." I started to furiously pedal because it really was time for Daddy to come home.

A Visit From Uncle Buddy

Willie Jimmerson was my father. His nickname was "Butterbean" a monicker given to him by his grandfather, Sol Jimmerson. This was given after an apparent accident in Papa Sol's car which landed him in a garden of (you guessed it) butterbeans! This nickname would follow my father throughout his entire life.

Daddy worked at a local lamp factory here in town. Although I never heard him say it, I believe he liked this job a lot more than his last job at the oil mill. Working at the mill is where he broke his leg while on the job. I remember those being some pretty rough days for us. As a matter of fact this was also the time when my mother took in ironing to bring in extra money for the house.

'Butterbean' was a tall guy with a real 1950s look about him. He wore a pencil thin moustache which stood out on his slightly dark caramel skin tone. At thirty-nine he was starting to gray just slightly, but it suits him well.

He's a good guy, a strict parent, and a person who can't abide in laziness. Daddy did not want to see you in front of the TV when he got home from work. It was better to be outside playing or better still working in the yard.

Knowing his aversion to idleness I always made it my business to watch for his car as it turned off Remmel onto Clay Street. It would be at that point that I'd get a broom in my hand and begin to sweep off the walkway in front of our house. For the record, this empty gesture never fooled my father.

Just as I got to my house I run into Mr. Carl Kingston who lived down the street from us. Mr. Carl and his very large family were long time residents on Clay Street. They were here when we moved into our house in 1962. He was the only grown man I knew at the time who didn't drive, but rode a bike or walked everywhere he went.

I get my bike put away around to the back of the house just in time to grab the broom. I head to the sidewalk in front of our house and start my pretend sweeping and looking out for daddy. I hadn't been at it very long when I spot the brown "Batmobile." That was daddy's old 1957 Buick that looked just like the Batmobile from Gotham City. We hated that car. It was too ugly for words!

Now with the Batmobile in sight, I really start to sweep the walkway. I couldn't see the car as it turned into the carport around back, but I knew that Daddy had seen me as he came down the street. I kept sweeping because I wanted to get full credit for working really hard.

When daddy comes in, he sees mama finishing his plate. On the menu were turnip greens and fried chicken which were favorites of his, especially when this dish was served with large pieces of onion.

Yea, 'Butterbean' loved his onion. He also loved to drink a tall glass of buttermilk with cornbread crumbled into it.

He would have this instead of the kool-aid with lemons we would be drinking.

Usually daddy sat down to eat first then the rest of us would be called. Mama was never seated until all of our plates were filled.

Today before sitting down for supper, daddy made his way to the front porch. He wanted to see if I was still sweeping off the walkway.

"Hey daddy, when did you get home?" I made sure that I wiped away a little fake sweat when I said that.

"Oh, a few minutes ago. I see you've been working very hard." Daddy had that slight smile on his face, the one that says "Girl, you might as well put that broom down cause you not fooling anybody!"

This was just one of many ways daddy used to let us know that we couldn't 'put one over on him'.

He was also known to come in and feel the sides of the TV set to see how warm it was. As he would put it, "I know y'all been here all afternoon sitting on your behinds and watching TV."

"Doris Marie, come on in and wash your hands. Your mama got supper ready." Daddy holds the door for me all the while he's still sporting that sly smile.

"Daddy, could I have some money? Tomorrow is the twenty-seventh, mama's birthday" I had that pleading look that only kids get when they have the slightest chance to play on their parent's sympathies.

"I can give you and Charlene three dollars each. You'll have to go in together to buy her present." Daddy handed me six dollars and instructed me to give Charlene her half when she got home.

Minutes later, Charlene could be heard coming in the backdoor. . . still singing off key. Her favorite song was "RESPECT" by Aretha Franklin. But she somehow always managed to get the words wrong. The song is supposed to go 'R-E-S-P-E-C-T find out what it means to me. Charlene sings R-E-S-P-E-C-T find 'it' out what it means to me. And she sang it like that every time!

"Charlene, come here" I motioned for her to follow me to our bedroom. "Look daddy gave us three dollars each to buy a present for mama's birthday".

I handed over her share of the money. "You want to go in together or do you want to buy on your own?" I was definitely hoping she wanted to share in the present buying. This way we might have some left over for ourselves.

"I have an even better idea. Let's get Velma to kick in then we can really buy a nice present and have some left over." Charlene was plenty eager to spend our older sister's money.

"Yeah, but If Velma helps out she will use most of her money and get most of the credit. You okay with that?" Charlene spent a few moments pondering the question.

"Well, we'll just have to make sure mama knows that we contributed too. We can do that by buying her a card AND putting our names on the gift." Well this was a problem that was easily solved.

We both breathed a small sigh of relief now that we had shifted that job off to Velma. We were certain that she would do it because it was for mama. . . otherwise we could forget it.

My sister and I washed up and then sat down to supper. The smells of mama's greens and fried chicken were calling our names.

The major attraction tonight was Mama's peach cobbler. Daddy was already seated at the table gorging huge slices of yellow onion with the turnip greens.

At first glance, my father didn't appear as someone with such an insatiable appetite. This evening he gulped down several pieces of chicken, two helpings of greens with large slices of yellow onion, a huge glass of buttermilk with cornbread and daddy still had room for cobbler!

Of course, at some point he would have to unbuckle his belt and loosen his pants to make room for everything.

This particular ritual was almost certain to be accompanied with one or more healthy burps. At this time daddy would always say the same thing "Whoa Lordy! That felt good!"

"Doris Marie, go and get your father the newspaper." I'm guessing mama couldn't wait for daddy's usual routine of leisurely reading the paper after supper. Daddy looks a bit surprised but doesn't question mama's actions.

After handing the paper over to Daddy, mama points to the article about Velma and waits for his reaction. Again, we can see that subtle smile on his face. We could tell that daddy approved of his eldest's child's accomplishments.

"Well, I guess that's alright. I'm happy for her." Daddy was a man of few words.

About this time we hear Velma's key turning in the front door. She's a bit late this evening which means she probably had to walk home.

"I'm home and I'm hungry!" Velma was in an unusually good mood for someone who had just walked about four blocks from work. My sister worked in the kitchen at Newport Hospital. Working in the kitchen or the laundry of the local hospitals and motels were jobs held by many young black women at that time.

"Come on back here and get your plate." Mama gets up and fixes Velma's plate. She didn't put much on it because my sister did not possess a huge appetite. She was tall and thin like our father but didn't possess his voracious appetite. Daddy used to call her "Thin Jean".

"Did you read NEWS ABOUT COLORED PEOPLE in this evening's paper? Mrs. March wrote a very nice article about you and Laura going to AM&N this fall." Mama was clearly excited about the newspaper article.

"Yeah, we read it at work. I gotta call Mrs. March and thank her for writing it." Velma was trying to be very humble but we knew she was bursting at the seams with pride.

"Personally I can't wait for you to go... 'cause I am going to get your room." Velma's bedroom wasn't bigger than ours, but she didn't share it with it anyone either. I had every intention of getting it when she left.

That is unless Mama and Daddy decided to give it to Charlene. After all, she was the next oldest. Either way I'd be getting a room by myself and that's really all that mattered.

"I don't care which one of you gets it, as long as you remember to get your narrow behind out of it when I come home. My oldest sister was basically a very nice person, but she could be quite territorial about her room.

"All I ask is that you remember home and how you were raised. I really don't want you traveling too far away from home once you have finished school." This was our father's way of saying that he was proud of Velma and that he would miss her.

All of a sudden the attention was taken away from our sister because of the loud commotion at our backdoor.

"Hey Butterbean, Hey Gurt! Didn't y'all hear me at the front door? I'm justa knockin' and no one came so I decided to come 'round back!"

It was Uncle Buddy. If he had called out to us instead of rapping on the door we probably would have heard him. Buddy Jimmerson was daddy's uncle from Augusta, Arkansas. He was without a doubt the loudest person on planet earth (and he'd give the Martians a run for their money too!)

Being so wonderfully loud was one of Uncle Buddy's trademarks and we all loved him for it. You generally heard him before you actually saw him. Every relative on daddy's side of the family could imitate Uncle Buddy. You weren't a real Jimmerson if you couldn't 'mark' him.

His other trademark was his fashion sense. None of us are quite certain just where Uncle Buddy did his shopping. We are equally uncertain of just when was the last time he shopped. His clothes had to be leftovers from a bye gone era.... like the Forties. He was known to wear any type of combinations stripes with plaids, polka dot purple shirt/yellow pants, and big bowties. He never met a color combo he didn't like.

"Uncle Buddy, come on in here. I guess we didn't hear you with the radio on in the living room and the fan on in the hallway. But come on in and pull up a chair. Want some supper?" Mama knew the answer to that question. Uncle Buddy was tall and skinny like daddy but his appetite was much bigger.

"Well, I guess I'll take a little bit. Sho' is smelling good. Whatcha got some turnip greens?"

"Yea, Uncle Buddy we got some greens and chicken. And some peach cobbler if you want some." IF he wanted some?! Mama must be kidding. Of course he wanted some. Even though, Uncle Buddy was talking a mile a minute, I could see that he was eyeballing my mother to make sure she piled his plate high.

"Buddy, ain't it kinda late for you to be out this evening?" Daddy knew that Uncle Buddy like most older people didn't like being away from their homes when it was getting late in the evening.

"I had to bring my gullfriend, Mrs Betsy Brown and one of her lady friends up here to visit someone. You know Mrs. Louella Simpson over on Second Street?"

"Didn't she have a stroke?" A question mama knew the answer to. That was another item we had just read in Mrs. March's column.

"Yeah, she had a light stroke, but she's fine now. You can hardly tell anything was ever wrong with her." Uncle Buddy was talking and chomping down on mama's good food at the same time. He didn't miss a beat either answering a question or eating that food. He was a pro.

"You know that Mrs. Louella is sister to Mrs. Betsy Brown." Uncle Buddy always referred to his 'gullfriend' as Mrs. Betsy Brown whenever he spoke about her.

"Buddy you still courting at your age?" Daddy gave us kids a little wink when he made that very personal inquiry.

"Yes suh, I sure am. I love me some Mrs. Betsy Brown. We been keeping company for now on seven years, ever since her husband died. I go over to her house to watch 'Gunsmoke' or the fights. Sometimes we sit on the front porch and enjoy a glass of ice tea. She's a lovely lady to have around. . . . even if she does make me go to church every Sunday!"

Uncle Buddy let out one of his big laughs and we joined in with him.

"Uncle Buddy, you mean Mrs. Betsy Brown got you going to church? You must really love her!" Daddy was really teasing him now. He knew Uncle Buddy wasn't exactly a church-going man.

"Where's Larry Wayne?" Uncle Buddy quickly shifted the subject by inquiring about our youngest brother who was out of town.

"He's been in Kansas City with BJ for three weeks. He'll be home before the Fourth." Uncle BJ was daddy's youngest brother and he lived in Kansas City, Kansas. He had come down the second week of summer vacation to pick up Larry and took him back to Kansas.

"How the rest of the chillun' doin'?" He could have asked us…… we were sitting right there but I guess he needed a quick and concise answer. It was about time to go and pick up Mrs. Betsy Brown.

Mama couldn't wait to answer this question. As it is with most parents, she wanted to brag a little on her child.

"Velma is getting ready to go to college this fall."

"You don't say?!" "Well, 'gull' listen here, you get all the education you can. Young folks these days don't have to work themselves to death in anybody's cotton field. You go on and get that education!" Older black folks loved to hear about the younger generation getting their education.

"Gurt, wrap me up some of that cobbler if you don't mind. I better get these old ladies and head on back to Augusta."

"Don't rush off." Mama did the polite thing of inviting the guest to stay longer, knowing that she really wants them to go. Even though she dearly loved Uncle Buddy, she'd had a long day and wanted desperately to sit down and relax a bit.

Uncle Buddy left out the front door with daddy trailing behind the two still deep in conversation.

"Okay, whose turn is it to wash dishes this week?" Asking this question was a mere formality on the part of my mother. I know this because she was looking straight at me when she asked.

"No need to ask. It's mine." I answered in a rather dead pan-like manner.

"Start on them right now. If you wait, you'll be too tired and will want to go to bed. And you know your father will drag you out of your bed to clean this kitchen tomorrow morning.

Boy, Gurt knew me all too well. Actually, I probably wouldn't mind doing the dishes tonight. It was still early and I had plenty of time before my favorite TV programs came on. Plus, WMPS was still coming in clearly on the radio.

The one good thing about doing the dishes (and trust me there is only ONE good thing) is having the kitchen radio to myself.

The radio in the kitchen unlike the big radio in the living room was always on either KNBY or WMPS. Mama kept it on KNBY our local station because she kept up with the local and state news. I was the person who usually dialed it to WMPS because I liked hearing Top Forty Hits. This was a mixture of all the popular sounds of the day.

I finally finished the dishes. The extra pan for the cobbler coupled with Uncle Buddy's visit put my plans back a few minutes. I was counting on going out again after supper. But it was definitely too late now.

The streets were about thirty minutes away from being illuminated from the several well placed lamp poles which aligned Clay Street. As it was with most parents of that time, we had to be home BEFORE those lights came on.

Even if I did go out and rode my bike over to Lillian's house, I couldn't spend anytime visiting. I'd have to turn right around and come back home within a matter of minutes. Nothing good ever happens when you're rushed for time.

The Candy Caper and Mama's Birthday Plans

It was getting late and time for our nightly routine. This routine, as most everything else in our household, had daddy at the helm as our leader. He was the first to eat, the first to bathe, and the first to go to bed for the evening. I, on the other hand, was almost always the last. Because as mama put it "That girl slo-pokes around for everything!"

Personally, I just liked having certain areas of the house all to myself even if it is just for a brief moment. When you come from a large family it's hard to find some personal space. So, whenever I could find some 'alone' time I took full advantage of it. Being the last person in the bathroom meant I wouldn't have anyone rushing me to finish. I could languish for as long as I chose without the inescapable banging on the door to hurry me along.

I especially liked getting the TV to myself. It appeared that I would get that chance this evening. Daddy was in the tub and mama was ironing.

Velma was on the phone and Charlene was in our room reading the latest Hit Parade Magazine. As a result, the TV was mine. PERFECT!

I looked around to see if it was clear to go on the porch to pick up my Baby Ruth and the cookies I'd gotten earlier from Mrs. McDaniel's store. The treats were still safely hidden in Daddy's toolbox or so I thought.

Quietly, I opened the front door. I bent down to open the toolbox and was immediately shocked. The toolbox was locked. Who could have done such a thing? I checked the box before I left for Lillian's and again when I returned.

And then I remembered that daddy had been on the front porch with Uncle Buddy earlier this evening. He most likely looked in it because he knows of my routine whenever I go to Mrs. McDaniel's store.

It's almost time for THAT GIRL and I need my treats! Just about that time daddy emerges from the bathroom dressed in his pajamas. I didn't hear him come into the living room, but there he stood.

"Looking for something?" Daddy had that 'gotcha' smile on his face.

"Uh, no sir. I . . . I was just checking to see if the screen door was locked." This was always a good excuse for going onto the front porch after hours.

"Well, don't be too quick to close the front door I need to get something out of the toolbox." Daddy's 'gotcha' smile got even bigger. He knew he had me and was just waiting to see what I was going to do.

"Daddy, you know you're not getting any tools this late at night. Besides, I think there's a fight on channel 13. You better hurry up before you miss it" I was really grasping at straws on this one.

First of all, I was out of place telling my father he could or could not do anything. Secondly, our TV couldn't get channel 13 unless the reception was cleared up by a good rain. Daddy didn't know this second part because he didn't watch TV enough to be aware of any reception problems.

"Your mama has been on me about putting up an extra shelf on the back porch." Daddy then calls to mama who was in the kitchen ironing.

"Gurthalean, I'm going to put up that shelf for you tonight." Daddy was trying to be slick. He knew if he got mama in on the joke it would seem more realistic.

Oddly enough, mama didn't answer. She knew daddy was up to something when he volunteers to do any kind of work after he's had his bath.

"Okay, Now let me look in here and get out my hammer". Daddy already had his key for the lock. He then proceeds to open up the toolbox only stopping momentarily to turn on the front porch light.

"Wait a minute, what do we have here? I guess Santa must be a little early. He's left me some candy and cookies. And as luck would have it, they're all my favorites: a delicious BABY RUTH and some chocolate chip cookies." He even licked his lips to add to the effect!

"Daddy, you know that's my candy! You not gonna eat that are you?" I had my best 'sad kid' look on my face.

"Willie, give that girl her candy. Doris Marie, you have to share that with your sister." She didn't specify which sister, but we all knew she meant Charlene. Velma had a job and could afford to buy her own junk food.

"And I've told you about keeping my change when I send you to the store, little girl!" Translation of the latter part of this sentence: DO IT AGAIN AND YOU WILL GET A WHOOPING!

"Charlene, come up here your sister got something for you!" Daddy was a little too anxious to give away my hidden treats.

Surprisingly, Charlene didn't want but a small portion. Generally, we have to split everything down the middle.

Once, mama even cut a 'Cracker Jack' box down the middle so that Charlene and I could share. My guess is my sister must have had too much cobbler at supper and was still quite full. This was reason number one why I didn't fill up on the dessert.

Soon after his 'award winning' performance, daddy spent a few minutes talking with mama in the kitchen. He polished off a small helping of cornbread and buttermilk and then went to bed.

The credits for THAT GIRL were rolling down the TV screen and BEWITCHED was next. I hoped that 'Uncle Arthur' would be on tonight. It was always funnier when he visited Darrin and Samantha, even though you could sometimes see the attached strings when he was floating objects through the air.

Suddenly the phone rings and it was Lillian. It was unlike her to call me at night especially during one of my favorite shows. So, I'm figuring this must be some really great gossip. . . and I was right.

"I thought you were coming back out after supper?" Lillian sounded a bit upset. Not angry upset, but more annoyed upset.

"Uncle Buddy came by for a visit and had supper with us. That took up all of my time. What's up?"

My Uncle's visit as an explanation would do because Lillian knew I couldn't just leave when I had company over, especially if its 'kin'.

"Wait a minute. Don't tell me I missed my boyfriend!" She wasn't kidding by much. Lillian always got a kick out of listening to Uncle Buddy talk.

"Did he bring Mrs. Betsy Brown?"

Lillian did her best Uncle Buddy impression while asking the question.

"I know you didn't call over here this time of the night to talk about Uncle Buddy and his 'gulfriend'. What's on your mind? Did you see your boyfriend, Gary?"

Lillian proceeds to tell me of how she and her mom saw Doll and Gary outside after supper. Lillian's mom went out every evening after supper to water her flower gardens. Mrs. Jarrett was quite proud of the flowers in front because they were the most colorful.

Her flower bed was filled with red and white roses and other beautiful summer perennials. In the back of the house were mostly Elephant ears. It didn't take much to keep them alive. But the flowers in the front had to be 'babied'.

It was Lillian's job to help water the flowers and pick up any paper in the yard. Lillian hated doing either one. She didn't mind being outside, she just hated working outside.

But as luck would have it, the young couple was outside and Mrs. Jarrett spotted them and walked over to engage the two in conversation. Lillian had a mix of emotions concerning the two.

On the one hand she felt a sense of familiarity having met them earlier in the day. But on the other hand she was somewhat embarrassed because of her little crush for Gary.

At first, the conversation was very general and cordial in a 'getting—to-know-you' kind of way. Once Gary learned of Mrs. Jarrett's roots in Alabama, the conversation turned quite intense.

Some very interesting news was revealed during the course of the conversation. Gary learned that Mr. and Mrs. Jarrett had participated in the Montgomery Bus Boycott in 1955.

This information was huge for Gary. He saw this as a major link to history right here next door to his mother-in-law. Both Gary and Doll were spellbound while Mrs. Jarrett told of the many acts of bravery exhibited by the everyday people who participated in the historic event.

After talking with Lillian my sisters and I had a powwow in the living room. We needed to discuss mama's birthday. Mama was in the kitchen fixing daddy's lunch pail for the next day. Daddy was in bed which meant we had to keep both the TV and our voices down low so he could get to sleep.

With Velma's money and our six dollars we had forty-six dollars for mama's birthday. My sister decided to buy her a nice, dressy outfit at JC Penny. Mama could probably wear the new ensemble to the big wedding at First Baptist on Sunday.

We decided to give mama an impromptu birthday party on the following day. Velma was responsible for the food and decorations. Charlene and I were instructed to get her sisters, Aunt Helen and Aunt Juanita and her two best friends Mrs. Louise Taylor and Mrs. Georgia McCoy to take her window shopping downtown. That was right up mama's alley, she loved to window shop. This would be too easy considering JC Penny and Van Atkins were mama's favorite places to shop.

That night while Mama had her bath, we made the necessary phone calls to set up the birthday arrangements.

The ladies agreed to the shopping arrangements. Mrs. Louise said that they would also take Mama to TED's LUNCHROOM for a quick bite. These last minute plans were working out quite nicely.

Now that the birthday event was in place, we watched TV a little while longer. We decided to watch PEYTON PLACE. Velma, Mama, and Charlene loved the show. I liked it enough but if I had the TV to myself and something else was on, I'd watch something else.

On mama's insistence, I decided to bathe while the others were involved with their program.

Even though summer had made its official arrival a few days ago, there was still a kind of cool, crispness in the air. This made for a very pleasant evening. Charlene had already put the fan in the window and this caused our bedroom to be pleasantly cool. The coolness also meant NO MOSQUITOES.

There are two words that can adequately describe Arkansas mosquitoes: MERCILESS and RELENTLESS!!

On a hot summer night mosquitoes would attack as though they had been in training for their mission all day.

We didn't have air conditioning during those early years on Clay Street. As a result, we spent the majority of those sweltering summer nights doing battle with those southern blood sucking 'skeeters.'

Speaking on one particularly steamy night, my mother gave a rather amusing description of our annoying 'friends.' She swore that the mosquitoes were so bad that they had 'prayer and church-meeting' in her ears!

By ten o'clock only mama and Velma were still stirring in the house. Since she didn't have to get up tomorrow, mama would stay up past ten to watch Channel Four News. Her nephew, Nathaniel Sammuel Brown was a marine stationed in Viet Nam. Because of this, mama tried to keep up with any and all news concerning the war.

Velma would also stay up for a little while longer talking on the phone to Elliot, her new boyfriend. Elliot Jackson, who was from Batesville, Arkansas, was a sophomore at AM&N and Velma was very much in love with him. They met at a Homecoming Dance last fall and apparently it was love at first sight for both of them.

Although unknown to either Charlene or me, Velma was making plans for Elliot to come down for mama's party tomorrow. Having him here for the party was okay with us because we all liked Elliot. Even daddy thought he was alright, and that was rare. Daddy usually hated all of Velma's boyfriends.

Chapter 2

Mrs. Louise Helps out with the Birthday plans
Tuesday, June 27

I woke up with the smell of bacon clouding my nostrils. As I lay there, I secretly wished that my body could follow the scent by floating away like they do in those MGM cartoons. This way I could immediately be seated at the table to enjoy the great breakfast mama had prepared.

After washing up, I head for the kitchen in a robotic-like stride. Mama has breakfast already prepared. She is seated at the table rereading yesterday's paper and drinking a hot cup of coffee while listening to the local news on KNBY.

"Happy Birthday, Mama." I gave her a big kiss on her jaw.

"We got you something really nice. You are going to be so surprised!" I was also going to be surprised because I had no idea what outfit Velma was going to buy for her.

"So, you're not going to tell me what it is?" Mama was still being playful while she piled the bacon, eggs, and biscuit bread onto my plate. She must have thought (and rightfully so) that I would be so entranced by the smells of breakfast, that I would readily spill the beans.

I held onto our planned party secrets, even though it wasn't easy.

The aroma of a "mama cooked" breakfast could easily loosen the tongue of any seasoned spy.

While we were eating, a familiar country song came on the radio. "May the bird of paradise fly up your nose!" These lyrics rumbled through the air as they did most mornings whenever Mama had the radio tuned to KNBY.

Charlene finally relinquishes her bed and stumbles into the kitchen singing along with the radio.

"Ooh sing it Charlene! I always knew you liked that country music!" She asked for that teasing. I mean she DID come into the kitchen singing the corniest song ever written.

"Little girl, leave your sister alone, because I've heard you singing that very song plenty of times." Leave it to Gurt to serve as peacemaker.

"Thanks, mama" Charlene playfully sticks out her tongue at me as if to say "See mama is on my side."

Before I get a chance to crack on Charlene once more, the phone rings. Velma promptly picked up the receiver as though she had anticipated the call. We could hear Mrs. Louise loud and clear through the receiver.

"Hey College girl, Let me talk to Gurt!" Velma hands the phone over to mama.

"Happy Birthday to you. Happy birthday to you." Mrs. Louise was belting out the birthday song loud and clear. She almost sounded as though she was in the room with us.

"Louise, I know you didn't call me this early in the morning just to sing happy birthday!"

"Now why you go and cut me off? I didn't get a chance to finish my beautiful song. I know you not trying to say I can't sing cause you know I can!" With that Mrs. Louise belted out one of signature boisterous laughs.

"No, I'm not trying to say you can't sing. You just took me by surprise with that 'caterwauling' or I meant to say 'beautiful singing' so early in the morning! But I do thank you for calling."

"Girl, you're a mess." Mrs. Louise was really enjoying teasing mama so early in the morning.

"What did the girls get you for your birthday?"

"The girls let ME cook THEM breakfast on MY BIRTHDAY. So, in a word the girls haven't gotten me anything for my birthday... yet." Mama made sure that she was staring at all of us when she said that.

"Well, Gurt, I tell you what. Let the girls clean the house while you and I do a little window shopping this afternoon. We can even go to Ted's Lunchroom for their special. How does that sound to you?"

Mama was about to offer up her usual reasons why she couldn't go. But before she could utter a word, Mrs. Louise 'beat her to the punch.'

"Now Gurt, It's your birthday. The girls can hold down the fort. They do it when you're at work don't they? Besides, you don't need money to window shop and I am paying for lunch."

"OK, Louise, you win. What time are you coming by?"

Mama gave in without much of a fight. She knew it was pointless to argue with Mrs. Louise once she had made up her mind about anything.

"I guess I'll come by around noon. That sound okay with you?"

"Yeah that sounds like a plan. I'll be ready and waiting." Mama sounded a little too excited about leaving us for a few hours.

While Mama and Mrs. Louise were making their plans for the afternoon, Velma motioned for Charlene and me to meet her in our bedroom.

As quietly as she could, Velma proceeded to inform us of her plans for mama's party. She was going to bake the cake before mama left. This way mama wouldn't suspect her of throwing a surprise party because she had already seen the cake.

Velma called her friend Laura Marks to come by and take her to Bausch and Long Jewelers. Daddy had purchased a 'mother's ring' there for mama a few weeks ago. Velma also had an outfit in mind. This is actually the reason why she was a little late on yesterday. She was scouting out outfits at Van Atkins and JC Penny.

I was starting to wonder why she needed me and Charlene at all. She had made all the important plans herself way before consulting with us.

All that's needed now was to get mama out of the house and back home by two o'clock. This way the party should be over by the time daddy got off work. A house filled with giggling women was the last thing daddy wanted to see when he came home from a hard day at work.

Velma gave Charlene and me each a dollar and fifty cents back which we quickly put away in our dresser drawer for safe keeping. She knew the 'free show' at the Strand Theatre was coming up on Friday and we would want some spending money. A dollar fifty cents in 1967 was big money. All we needed for the free show was about fifty cents for snacks and a ticket from one of the local businesses for the admission. The movie was free.

It was almost eight twenty and definitely time for us to start our morning routine. This consisted of the usual pattern of cleaning our rooms, cleaning the house, and washing dishes. The latter was my job since I was on kitchen duty this week.

But as luck would have it, by the time I got back to the kitchen, mama was finishing off the dishes and was about to put on a pot of white beans. I would have stopped her since it was her birthday, but she was singing. Listening to your mother sing while in the kitchen cooking is probably one of the most soothing sounds in the world.

Much to our dismay, mama had a chore for Charlene and me. We had to go out to our garden and pick 'a mess of' okra. A job I hated. First of all, picking okra made me itch something fierce. Second you could easily run up on a snake or a slimy frog. Although I had never actually run up on a snake in the garden, I had seen my share of frogs . . . ugh!!

Fortunately, my love for the taste of fried okra surpassed my disdain for the job of obtaining it.

We were also told to bring in several large ripe tomatoes. Yummy! It is a known fact that few vegetables can compete with the taste of a juicy ripened tomato, when it accompanies a great summer meal.

After bringing in the vegetables from the garden, mama said it was okay for Charlene and me to go visit with our friends. We gave a quick goodbye then hurriedly scattered off in different directions. With our absence mama would have the house to herself for a while. We didn't know it at the time, but this was probably the best birthday gift mama could have gotten that day.

Charlene headed for Calhoun Circle. We had a set of twin cousins who lived there and she mentioned earlier that she would probably go by there. Charlene was very family oriented. She recognized all relatives; immediate and distant. It didn't matter if you were an 8th cousin twice removed. You were her 'kin'!

I biked over to Lillian's house. When I got there, I headed to the side entry. This door led directly to the Jarrett's den. I figured that Lillian would most likely be there. I guessed correctly because there she was sitting in front of the TV playing with Bella, the world's laziest dog. After five minutes of playing fetch with Bella, YOU had to 'go and get the stick' because he was done for the day!

The door was open so I went right in.

"Hello Mrs. Jarrett" I didn't immediately see her, but I could hear her stirring about in the next room.

"Hey there, Doris Marie. I hear today is your mama's birthday. Tell her Happy Birthday for me, okay?"

"I will. We are having a small surprise party for her this afternoon. You should come by and have some cake with us." I knew Mrs. Jarrett probably wouldn't come. She generally kept a low profile during the summer. Lillian says that her mom rested the first part of the summer and then they vacationed the second part of the summer.

"Oh Sweetie, I'm going to relax around the house and tend to my flowers. But you make sure you give your mama my best, you hear?" I assured Mrs. Jarrett that I would relay her birthday wishes.

"Let's go over to Sheritha's house. If she's not on punishment maybe she can ride bikes with us."

I had ulterior motives to my bike riding adventure. It was midday and still not too terribly hot outside so this made it great for bike riding. In the south you learn to take advantage of any summer day when the temps run even slightly below 90 degrees.

"Can you wait a few minutes? I 'm watching THE DATING GAME and there's a black girl on. I hadn't immediately noticed how engrossed Lillian was to the program being displayed on the screen.

Black people on TV? Yeah, we would have to wait to ride our bicycles. Black people on TV in the 1960s was still a bit rare, so whenever we caught someone who looked like us on a major program we felt obliged to watch.

I settled on the floor with Lillian and Bella to watch the end of the show. The young lady was quite attractively dressed in her lavender and white psychedelic colored two piece suit. The top was sleeveless and stopped just past her belly button. The bottom was a mini skirt which matched the top's psychedelic print. The white 'go-go' boots she wore were a nice compliment to her outfit.

Her 'mod' style was further accented by her deep ebony skin, short afro hairstyle, and lavender hoop earrings. I was glad that I was at Lillian's so that I could see the outfit in color. We loved the outfit the young lady wore and complained that it was near impossible to find something so trendy in our little small town.

We also agreed that it didn't matter anyway because there is no way our parents would let us wear something so daring. That was definitely an outfit for a much older girl.

We left soon after the program ended.

While pedaling our way down Remmel Street we could see Mr. Inez Robertson who was leaning against his car on the passenger's side in front of Craft Funeral Home. I knew Mr. Inez a little better than Lillian because years ago he had worked with daddy at the oil mill.

I wouldn't say that he and daddy were close friends. But I do remember seeing him talking with my father in our front yard on several occasions.

We lessened our speed a bit as we neared Mr. Inez. As we approached him we could hear and see Mr. Inez doing something that bewildered us. . . . he was crying.

At this point, both Lillian and I started to walk with our bikes as we came even closer to the grieving parent. It didn't seem right somehow to whiz past him as he was deep in his personal torment.

He had his handkerchief out and was wiping away a continuous stream of tears all the while crying out "Why MY BOY, Lord?!" "He was my only child!" Mr. Inez's son had been a soldier serving in Vietnam.

I had spoken to Mr. Inez on many occasions but all I could muster up at this time was a quiet ". . . . I'm sorry about your son, Mr. Inez."

He didn't respond to my weak attempt at trying to put him at ease. As a matter of fact, he didn't acknowledge our presence at all. Later in the evening when I discussed his behavior with mama, she completely understood. Mama said that Mr. Inez was drowning in his grief. It wasn't that he was ignoring Lillian or me, but that he couldn't see anybody at that time.

Neither Lillian nor I knew what to do. We were just kids and had no real idea as to how to console him. So, we decided to move on. . . . our only known option.

For the first minute or so we didn't say a word to each other. I guess we were in a kind of state of shock.

Finally, Lillian broke the silence with the awaiting question about Mr. Inez's son.

"Did you know his son?" You could see the look of genuine concern on her face.

"Yeah, His name is Carlos"

I tried to keep a straight face and not show any emotion. It was all I could do to keep from tearing up. Carlos was the joy of his parents' lives.

"Why haven't I ever seen him around y'all's house?" *Lillian prided herself in being an honorary member of our family. Consequently, she assumed that anyone we knew she should also know.*

"Carlos has been gone for about six years. He went to college for a while then dropped out to join the army. This was his second time fighting in Vietnam. I feel so sorry for Mr. Inez."

After a few more moments of silence, Lillian posed another question. "Doris Marie, have you ever seen a grown man cry before?"

"I saw my father cry once when his sister died. He didn't know I saw him. When my uncle called and told him about the death, daddy handed the phone to mama and walked outside. He got the water hose and started to wash his car, but we could see the tears rolling down his face."

I told Lillian that we probably shouldn't continue this conversation once we got to Sheretha's house. She agreed even though I offered up no reason as to why we shouldn't talk about the funeral home incident.

We climbed upon our bicycles and proceeded on to our friend's house.

Meet Bobby Joe Walker

We were about to turn onto Sheritha's street when my self-appointed boyfriend since 5th grade, Bobby Joe Walker, shows up on his bike. Ever since we were paired together as angels in a Christmas Pageant, Bobby Joe has proclaimed his undying love for me. This wouldn't be so bad if he didn't do so in THE most annoying ways possible!

"Hello Doris Marie! I haven't seen you since the last day of school. I know you miss me!" *As usual he is talking to me as if I was standing six feet away from him.*

"Bobby Joe Walker how many times do I have to tell you that we are NOT boyfriend and girlfriend. Not now! Not ever!" *I had to stop my bicycle at this point so I could use hand gestures and facial expressions to emphasis my point.*

"Girl, you might as well stop playing. You know you love me. Now give me a kiss." At this point Bobby Joe closes his eyes and puckers up his lips. Ehew!

Suddenly, I had a vision of holding up Lillian's dog to those waiting lips. I would have done it too if that lazy mutt had been anywhere nearby. This would serve Bobby Joe right for being so irritating.

At this point Lillian is about to fall off her bike because she's laughing so hard.

Bobby Joe still has his eyes closed so Lillian and I used the opportunity to escape and continued on to Sheritha's house.

Unfortunately I didn't make a clean getaway. Bobby Joe opened his eyes and once again screamed out his love for me as Lillian and I pedaled our way down the street.

"I LOVE YOU DORIS MARIE AND WE ARE GOING TO GET MARRIED!"

The funny thing is that this is not the first time this knucklehead has done something like this.

Once I made the mistake of riding bikes with him around the neighborhood. When we rode down Clay Street and on to my house, he yelled out something equally embarrassing.

To my horror both mama and daddy were outside working in the yard. Daddy still teases me about that. Every once and awhile when I least expect it I will hear:

MR. WILLIE, I BROUGHT YOUR DAUGHTER HOME! I swear that boy is ten different kinds of annoying.

In a way I was kind of glad we ran into Bobby Joe. His loud mouth helped to take my mind off of Mr. Inez's grief.

By the time we get to Sheritha's house, the unmistakable smell of barbeque is filling the air. Mr. Curtis was in the back yard cooking a variety of meats and vegetables on an open grill.

Curtis Mills was Mrs. Carmen's boyfriend and not a favorite of Sheritha's.

It wasn't that he was a bad person who mistreated or disrespected her or her mom. Mr. Curtis went out of his way to be nice to Sheritha's family. And it wasn't that he was lazy and didn't help out around their house. He worked full time at the steel mill and part time as a barber in Mr. Marvin Reed's Barber Shop.

The main reason Sheritha didn't like Mr. Curtis was because he wasn't Pete Wilson, her father. Sheritha was certain that no one could take the place of her father and she still held out hope of him coming back to the family. Mrs. Carmen has told Sheritha on any number of occasions that she needs to get that thought out of her head.

Mr. Pete and Mrs. Carmen divorced several years ago when Sheritha was about eight or nine. Even though her father now lived in Chicago, He and Sheritha were still quite close. He would come down several times during the year to visit with Sheritha and other close relatives in the area. Even though she didn't dislike Mr. Curtis, she still would rather have had her father there barbecuing with her family.

"Doris Marie, did I hear someone propose marriage to you a few moments ago?

Sheritha's Aunt Theola was a sort of shy person who didn't always have a lot to say. But she did have a wicked sense of humor. It seems that just moments ago Aunt Theola was in her bedroom and heard (along with everybody else in the neighborhood) Bobby Joe's shocking proposal.

"Well, do I need to buy a new dress for the special occasion?" Aunt Theola was really enjoying this.

"No ma'am, I can't stand that boy. He's always saying something stupid. And he thinks I like him just because one day in 5th grade we had to be angels together in a Christmas play. . . eehew!"

"Alright keep complaining and the next thing you know, Butterbean will be walking you down the aisle." Now Mother Ann has tagged in on the teasing.

"Alright that's enough of y'all teasing Doris Marie. Come here baby and give me a hug." Thank God Mrs. Carmen came to my rescue. I hurried over to those welcoming open arms.

"Come on now and get some of this food" Mrs. Carmen motioned for Lillian and me to sit down at their picnic table. They had all kinds of goodies: potato salad, banana pudding, baked beans, slaw, hot dogs, barbeque chicken and grilled green tomatoes. . . . EVERYTHING!!

If I didn't have to get back home for mama's party, nothing on that picnic table would have been safe from my enormous appetite.

But I had to save room for the birthday treats waiting for me back home.

"I have to get back home in a few minutes. We are having a surprise birthday party for my mother. I just came by to see if Sheritha could come to my house this afternoon for a few minutes." Out of the corner of my eye I could see Sheritha pleading with her mom. Although she didn't speak, she was mouthing the words "please, please" while motioning with her hands in a 'prayer' like manner.

"Okay, Okay, you can go. But remember I need you back home by four o'clock, Miss Thing! Am I clear on that?"

Miss Carmen had to yell the last part because as soon as she said, "Okay you can go" Sheritha had jetted away.

"Hey Sheritha, did you hear a certain person's boyfriend a few minutes ago? A certain person got another marriage proposal from her main squeeze."

Lillian's little known 'mean streak' was making a rare appearance.

"Yeah, I heard him. This IS Bobby Joe Walker we're talking about. He's so loud, when he speaks the Martians put on ear muffs!"

I was really starting to hate Bobby Joe Walker. . . that big-tooth rat!

"For the record, Aunt Theola and Mother Ann both said that they would sing at your wedding."

"That's okay Sheritha. Besides I'm sure they're saving their voices for your mama's wedding to Mr. Curtis."

That was mean of me. Almost immediately, I could see a slight hurtful look appear on her face. After all, I know how sensitive that subject was with Sheritha. This was a poor choice of words on my part and certainly not the time for playing the 'dozens.'

"I'm sorry, Sheritha." I hoped I delivered those words with the honest sincerity that I was feeling. After all, she was only joking about Bobby Joe.

"That's okay. Girl I know you don't like no Bobby Joe Walker. Y'all wanna go to Sloan's Grocery to buy some Red Hots?" She didn't seem to be as hurt as I'd thought.

"Naw, I don't want to go down Remmel right now." Lillian had such a serious scowl on her face that Sheritha gave me a very puzzling and inquisitive gaze.

"Did y'all run into Emma Jean and her bunch?" Sheritha voiced the most probable reason for our needed but unexplained detour of Remmel Street.

"No, it wasn't Emma Jean. You know how you have to pass by Craft Funeral Home sometimes." Lillian was trying to set up the best picture in Sheritha's mind.

"We pass by Crafts all the time. What's the big deal?" Sheritha's face had a look of impatience.

I decided to fill Sheritha in on the rest of the explanation.

"Today Mr. Inez was standing out front of Crafts . . . and he was crying. His son, Carlos, was killed in Vietnam." Sheritha's face had a look of disbelief. I immediately regretted telling her, but I thought she would hear about it sooner or later anyway.

It seems that no one had heard of Carlos' death. But I'm certain that before sunset every section south of Remmel Park will have heard of the loss. Mr. Inez's son was killed in a place thousands of miles away and now his body was home for its final resting place

"President Johnson should hurry up and end this stupid war!"

I wasn't surprised by this response of Sheritha. Her uncle Harold, Mrs. Carmen's twin brother, was killed in Mississippi several years ago. This was a loss that very nearly destroyed her family. Mama said that it was the strength of Mother Ann and her Aunt Theola that kept them together.

Sheritha was very fond of this uncle so any discussion about death could easily upset her.

Suddenly Sheritha did something completely unexpected.

She turned her bike around and headed back to her house.

"I'll try to come by later, Doris Marie. I need to go talk to Mother Ann.

Although, I had some idea why Sheritha was heading home after hearing the news about Carlos, I wasn't sure if Lillian knew.

"I didn't mean for her to get so upset! Why was she upset?"

Lillian as usual needed to make sense out of a somewhat confusing situation. It was her nature.

"I'm surprised that Sheritha hadn't told you."

"Told me what?" A deeply puzzled look had formed on Lillian's face.

"Sheritha's Uncle Harold was killed in Mississippi. He was Mrs. Carmen's twin brother. It happened a little before you moved here. This is why I didn't want to talk about it when we first got there."

"Doris Marie, I really wish you had told me this before I opened my big mouth!" Lillian was visibly upset with me mostly because her words had caused so much discomfort in Sheritha.

"If Bobby Joe hadn't been bothering me so I probably WOULD have remembered to tell you." "I'm sorry Lillian, but I'm sure Sheritha probably figured out that you didn't know about her uncle."

Mama's Birthday Party Surprise

By the time we got back to my house Lillian seemed to be in much better spirits. We parked our bikes in the front yard and went inside. There was mama and her friends sitting and watching their favorite soap DARK SHADOWS. Lillian and I both knew to enter quietly with very quick and low "hellos" to everyone. All kids know that when the 'soaps' are on we are not to disturb. . . . .especially if it's DARK SHADOWS.

"Hello everyone" Lillian and I spoke quickly and moved even quicker.

"Hello ladies now y'all gonna have to go to another room or back outside We are trying to watch our story."

Mama's voice was pleasant but stern. Translation: Hello, we're glad to see you, but move you're in front of the TV and Barnabas Collins is on.

After making our way to the kitchen, we found Velma and her boyfriend, Elliot, hidden away in a corner and embraced in a very passionate kiss. Lillian was tickled by the exhibition, but this was old hat for me.

"Y'all are suppose to be getting the food ready for mama's party, not back here slobbering all over each other!"

"The food is ready. And just where have you been? I thought you were going to help out." Velma was just showing off in front of Elliot.

She really didn't want my help. As she would put it I would just get in the way.

Just then Velma asks Lillian and me to get the food out of the refrigerator and help to set up the table for the party.

"There are tuna fish sandwiches, and two pitchers of lemonade in the refrigerator. Be careful now, because there is also a birthday cake and a sheet cake in there too. I got the sheet cake at Kroger"

Well, I guess she could use some help after all. Charlene had arrived by this time and volunteered to help by putting out the chips and dip.

Before putting out the food, Velma placed the prettiest red lace table cloth that she picked up at Fred's Dollar store onto the kitchen table. It wasn't expensive but it did add a real flair to the festivities.

The table looked quite inviting after setting it up with all the party favors.

We begin to sing the Birthday song and Elliot quickly exits to gather up mama and escorts her and her friends to the kitchen.

My mother is a rather shy person and all this attention directed her way was a little embarrassing to her. After a while she settled in and allowed everyone to shower her with all the love and attention she deserved. The party guests were instructed to take their food and drinks into our dining room where they could visit comfortably. I don't know when I've seen my mother have so much fun. Velma had done a fantastic job picking out her outfit. It was a dusty rose two piece skirt set. The top had a cowl type collar with a bow centered just beneath it. She even found a matching purse and gloves.

As stunning as the ensemble was this was not the item that got Gurthalean all choked up. It was the beautiful Mother's ring which had stones for April, September, November, and July representing all four of her children. When Mama saw that, the waterworks started and it spread to all the ladies in the room. Fortunately the tears didn't last for too long and the ladies resumed their delightful afternoon of revelry.

The party was a huge success and after about an hour and a half mama's guests started to leave. It was near perfect timing because it was getting close for daddy to come home from work.

Since Velma had put the party together practically all by herself, Charlene and I cleared away the party favors. Lillian would have helped but Mrs. Jarrett called for her to come home after about thirty minutes into the party.

We definitely didn't mind cleaning up after the party because we could eat some of the leftover treats. Mama had already made sure that daddy had some cake and ice cream saved for him in the fridge.

Charlene was in the middle of telling me about her encounter with Emma Jean and her bunch when we heard some familiar voices at the front door.

"Happy Birthday, Mama!" It was Larry Wayne, Uncle BJ, and Aunt Lorzee at the door. Apparently, Uncle BJ left out early this morning to get Larry Wayne home for mama's birthday.

Now the day WAS perfect because Gurt's baby was home!

"That boy worried me to death all last night about getting here for your birthday! And if HE wasn't worrying me Butterbean was calling me and worrying me. He wanted his boy home for your birthday."

"When did he call you?" Apparently daddy had been calling Uncle BJ and reminding him of mama's impending birthday without her knowledge.

"Happy Birthday, Gurt." Aunt Lorzee gets a chance to offer up her well wishes.

"Now you know your birthday was only a part of it. Butterbean just wanted his boy home. I'm surprised he let him stay as long as he did!"

Aunt Lorzee was daddy's younger sister and lived in Memphis. She had the uncanny ability to both irritate and tickle daddy at the same time, which she did often!

While mama and Aunt Lorzee talked, Uncle BJ and Larry Wayne went to the kitchen.

"Hey, girls where's MY birthday cake? Y'all didn't know Me and Gurt were born on the same day did you?"

Uncle BJ was the 'oldest' young man I knew. His movements and manner of speaking seemed to be that of someone in their fifties and not their twenties. I think he acts like an old man sometimes just to get a laugh out of us. If that's true then he's doing a bang up job 'cause he cracks us up all the time.

"Hey Uncle BJ, I guess y'all got tired of ol' big head here" Charlene was the first to greet Uncle BJ, who was without question her favorite relative.

"Naw, He could have stayed much longer if he wanted, but he wanted to get home. Plus Butterbean wanted him home ASAP."

Uncle BJ and Larry Wayne both had seated themselves at the table.

"Girls, I wasn't kidding about that cake!" For a man who was rather small in stature Uncle BJ could do some serious damage with a knife and fork.

"Charlene, fix your uncle a plate." Mama took time out from her conversation with Aunt Lorzee to shout instructions from the living room.

"BJ, we got some greens and cornbread in the refrigerator. Now, you are welcome to that and birthday cake and any leftover from the party". Mama always wanted to make sure that everyone had plenty to eat. Of course Larry Wayne was already stuffing his face with cake and sandwiches.

"Gurt, I already got the girls warming up some food for me. Lorzee, come on back here and get you some of Gurt's food."

"I'll get some in a few minutes. You go ahead and load up." Presently, Aunt Lorzee was too busy getting caught up with mama.

"Is that Velma's new boyfriend? He looks nice."

Aunt Lorzee had a very approving look on her face.

"They met at a dance at AM&N last year. Velma went down there to spend the weekend with some friends. They seem to be pretty serious about each other."

"What does Butterbean have to say about this?" Aunt Lorzee was expecting mama to give this big speech about how daddy didn't like him.

"They get along pretty good. I guess because the first time Elliot came by to see Velma, he bent Willie's ear for a good thirty to forty-five minutes."

Elliot left around eight-thirty. He and Velma had been forced to visit on the front porch while my parents and our company sat in the living room. He would have stayed longer but the mosquitoes ran him off saving daddy the trouble of doing that himself.

Uncle BJ and Aunt Lorzee stayed and visited with us on into the night and didn't leave for Memphis until around ten thirty the next day. I think part of the reason for the lengthy visit was because Uncle BJ was thoroughly tired from all that driving. Plus he had to sleep off the virtual feast he'd consumed the night before.

This was just fine with us as we loved it when daddy's folks visited. Charlene was especially fond of Uncle BJ who always managed to make her laugh and just feel generally good about herself.

Plus this gave daddy and Uncle BJ a chance to visit a bit longer. The two didn't get together that often so they wanted to make good use of this meeting.

It was clear that of all the gifts, friends, and relatives of the day, mama was most proud and happiest with the arrival of her "baby boy".

Larry Wayne coming home was the best present of all. This way mama had more time to spend with him before she had to go back to work.

Seeker Of The Truth

Even I was happy to have our little brother home. Besides being a pretty good kid, he was without a doubt the most gullible person on earth.

I mean you could tell Larry Wayne almost anything and he would believe you. The key of course is to keep a straight face and have a relatively plausible story.

This brings me to my most favorite Larry Wayne story. Mrs. Sheila Thornton was a lady who had a boarding house and lived down the street from us. Most of the people who rented there passed in and out of the neighborhood without much notice from anyone.

That was until a rather odd-looking, deeply dark-skinned fellow moved into Mrs. Sheila's establishment. He had salt and pepper kinky hair which grew down to his shoulders. Over his somewhat tattered jeans he wore a burlap caftan-like garment. He kept the top tied with a rope about his waist. The leather sandals worn completed his ensemble and gave him a 'biblical' look.

Honestly, he resembled a Black Jesus. That's what I thought of every time I saw him.

The first time I saw this resident of Mrs. Sheila's I was sitting on the front porch steps with Larry Wayne. We were eating ice cold Sip Dips from Mrs. McDaniel's Store on an unusually warm day right before summer vacation of this year.

Suddenly, and seemingly out of nowhere the Black Jesus was approaching our house on his way to the store. As he passed by he stopped momentarily to speak to us.

"Hello, little ones and how are you today?" He delivered those lines in an almost Shakespearean-like tone. After speaking, he proceeded onto the store.

Needless to say, Larry Wayne looked at me and I looked at him in complete astonishment. We did however manage to blurt out a very weak, 'Hello' before the Black Jesus disappeared from our sight.

"Doris Marie, who was that?" Larry Wayne was still a bit stunned at the unusual appearance of the stranger.

Now, I know I said that I THOUGHT he looked like Black Jesus. I knew that he wasn't Jesus……. black or white. But, I couldn't resist the urge to mess with my baby brother's all too gullible head.

"Larry Wayne, I can't believe you don't know who that is. Who does he look like?"

"I don't know what you're talking about, girl! He doesn't look like anybody I know."

"Uh, yes he does. He has long hair that's thick like lamb's wool, he's wearing a robe AND he's wearing sandals………He's Jesus!"

"Jesus is not black!" Larry Wayne was very defiant on this one.

"How do you know what color Jesus is? Have you ever seen him?" I'm really having to bite my lower lip a little to keep from laughing.

"Doris Marie you are going to Hell for saying such things and I'm gonna tell Mama!"

"M A M A! M A M A! And there he goes doing what little brothers and little sisters are so famous for… blabbing on you to your parents!

Minutes later Mama appears on the front porch with a towel still drying the dish with the apples, bananas, and oranges etched in the pattern.

Just as she was about to "bless" me out, the gentleman in question appears again as he exits Mrs. McDaniel's store.

"Good afternoon, Ma'am. How are you on this blessed day?" Again the 'Black Jesus' momentarily stops and converses with my mother.

"Good afternoon, Sir. I'm fine and thank you for asking."

I could clearly see that although Gurt was speaking to the gentleman her facial expression gave way to an inquisitive mind.

"Aren't you rooming there at Mrs. Sheila's Boarding House? Finding everything okay over there?"

"Yes, Ma'am, Mrs. Sheila is a lovely person and the accommodations are quite acceptable."

With that the Black Jesus turned and made his way back to the boarding house. He moved as though he hadn't a care in world while he carried his meager sack of groceries from the store.

"Mama, Is that man Jesus? Doris Marie said he was."

"No, Larry Wayne, that man is NOT Jesus. Doris Marie, stop telling your brother such ridiculous things." Mama was smiling a little while getting on my case about lying to Larry Wayne. I think that after seeing the caftan wearing gentleman, she was probably thinking the same thing!

This would not be our last encounter with the mirror image of the 'Man from Galilee.'

Chapter 3

A Killing in the Backyard Wednesday, June 28

Wednesday, the day after mama's birthday, arrived with the usual breakfast smells flowing from the kitchen. Of course, the first person I see when I entered the kitchen was Larry Wayne. He was chowing down the bacon, eggs, pancakes, and sausages Mama had cooked for him. I'm not sure, but I thought I saw sparks flying from his knife and fork. It had become a running joke around the house that Larry Wayne had an appetite much like "Jethro" on the BEVERLY HILLBILLIES.

Today would have come and gone without much notice had it not been for "A Killing in the Backyard."

My father had a real obsession with keeping our lawn mowed and the hedges cut. It was our job to keep the yard free of paper and other clutter. On this particular afternoon, daddy came straight in from work and started in on the yard. Mama had already gotten Charlene and me to pick up any paper or large twigs which could hamper the mowing.

Soon Daddy was hard at work moving the old yellow push mower up and down our backyard. He went first around some mulberry vines in the middle of our yard then onto a small apple tree in the back. Trouble didn't arise until he made his way to the back fence. Here is where he spotted one of the biggest snakes he'd seen since he lived in the country.

A rather large brown snake (at least five feet long) had wrapped itself around our back fence. Upon spotting the slithering brown menace, my father immediately rushed back to the house for his shotgun. Daddy had two shotguns on a rack in his and mama's bedroom. It had been a fixture on the wall for so many years that it was hardly noticeable by any of us in the house. However, it was a source of great interest to all the male cousins of the family. They were always asking about Uncle Willie's guns and what he planned to do with them. Even Larry Wayne was intrigued by the shotguns hanging there on the wall..

After grabbing one of the shotguns from the rack, daddy raced to find the unwelcome backyard guest. To his delight (because Daddy had few chances to use that shotgun) the snake hadn't moved far from the fence. He had wound his way to the far corner of the fence where he was well hidden within some rather tall grass.

Moving with the precision of an African big game hunter, Daddy carefully tracked down our reptilian friend. Apparently, the slithering menace had mistakenly thought itself safely camouflaged amidst the grass.

Quietly and with great accuracy, daddy cocked the shotgun and aimed it straight at the neck of the serpent. Within a matter of seconds he blasts the brown predator to snake heaven!

Of course, this brought out neighbors. Hearing a gun being fired off was quite unusual and the source and reason had to be investigated.

As the neighbors started to gather in and around our back yard, Daddy proudly held up the snake in his two hands. He presented the body of the snake in one hand and the severed head in the other.

This was an immediate source of fascination and amazement for the little fellas of the neighborhood.

"Mr. Willie you killed that snake?!"

"Man look at that snake Mr. Willie killed!"

"Yeah look at the shotgun! He blasted that snake!"

"Willie, what you gonna do with that snake?" Mr. Chuck had appeared from out of the crowd to witness the event.

"Well, Mr. Chuck I wasn't planning on doing anything with it except burn it with some other trash. Why you asking? You want it?"

Daddy was being a bit mischievous in his questions. He knew what Mr. Chuck was probably going to do with it. . . . ...skin it and hang it on his front porch. It would fit right fine along with the other two snake skins he had (one of which was a rattlesnake!)

Mr. Chuck was about to answer, when Mrs. McDaniel came out of her store with camera in hand.

"Butterbean, hold up that snake again I want to take your picture and hang it up in the store."

Well, what did she say that for?! Certainly he would let her take his picture and hang it in the store. Better still, maybe someone from the NEWPORT INDEPENDENT would hear about it and place his picture in the paper. Small town papers thrive on that kind of thing.

Every summer there was always the obligatory picture of someone who had killed a snake on their property. The second most popular picture would be of someone who had grown an unusually shaped or extremely large potato or tomato.

The excitement soon died down after Mrs. McDaniel had taken Daddy's picture and Mr. Chuck had gotten the snake carcass. Daddy finished off the yard and came into the house to have his supper. The snake story continued to be big news for the remainder of the evening and for days to come.

Daddy didn't tire of telling the story and Larry Wayne and his goofy little friends loved hearing about it. Every chance he got, Larry Wayne was showing off (from a safe distance of course) the rifle that ended the life of our unwelcomed slithering guest.

The picture was published in the paper and Mama taped it to the refrigerator. This just did our father all the good. Every time he'd pass by the refrigerator, he would comment on how handsome and brave he was.

Unfortunately, several weeks later an even larger chicken snake was killed behind our school gymnasium. This encounter along with the Bob Hope shaped potato grown by a local farmer completely overshadowed Daddy's backyard escapade.

Oh Well, there's always next year!

CHAPTER 4

Aunt Helen Meets the Seeker of the Truth
Thurs. June 29

A thunderstorm rumbled and roared its way through Newport on Wednesday night. The window fan in our bedroom helped to pull in all the crisp, fresh air which always followed a summer downpour. The air was so inviting that it made our beds feel very cozy and all but impossible to relinquish on such a cool morning. A heavy rain always made for the most comfortable night of sleeping.

It was still raining pretty hard when mama dragged us out of bed. There would be no bike riding or outdoor activities this morning. Until the rain ended we'd be inside.

After eating a hearty meal, we went about the business of completing our morning chores.

With everyone having an assigned job and working very hard, we always finished in record time. This left time to find something great to watch on TV. Since it was raining (which always made reception better), all three stations would come in clearly.

Before the advent of cable we relied on two things to have clear channels on our television. One thing was turning the outdoor antenna in just the right position and the other was a cleansing rain from Mother Nature. Today we had the latter of the two, now we could see reruns of some of our favorite sit-coms.

It's too bad that it wasn't the weekend. Saturdays and Sundays were great days for watching old movies. Channel Three showed the best old movies which were my mother's and my favorite. We both had our most cherished movie stars. Mama was a fan of Lena Horne and Barbara Stanwyck, while I favored Bette Davis. An old movie from the forties on a rainy afternoon coupled with a huge bowl of freshly popped corn was my idea of sheer bliss.

There were no movies on this afternoon, but we did find reruns of Andy Griffith and Dick Van Dyke along with a couple of game shows. Mama had made a pitcher of lemonade and Charlene popped the popcorn. Oh Yeah, we were in hog heaven!

After a while, the refreshing air from the open windows paired with our popcorn filled stomachs made everyone quite sleepy. As a result, we made pallets on the floor and caught a brief nap in the mid afternoon.

Later in the afternoon the sun gingerly peeked out and slowly pushed away the grey and white clouds. This brought the neighborhood kids out in droves to splash around in mother natures' mud filled, mini pools.

All around the neighborhood you could find boys racing bikes through the rainwater and purposely drenching anyone within range. Older siblings guided younger ones safely through puddles. It was amusing to hear little ones giggling and then crying from the uncomfortable feeling of mud oozing between their tiny toes.

The cooler temperatures after a summer rain, was also great porch sitting weather. Today's soothing temperatures summoned the arrival of mama's sister, Aunt Helen. She and Uncle William lived around the corner from us on Lake Street.

Aunt Helen was a tall, caramel skinned woman with dark but not completely black hair. She always kept her hair 'laid'. . . never a strand out of place. With her few extra (well placed) pounds, the word 'voluptuous' could easily be used to describe her. Her shapely figure coupled with the small mole situated on the lower right side of her nose gave her that classic Hollywood 1950s look.

She was always dressed quite nicely no matter what time of day or occasion. Mama used to say that Aunt Helen was always 'the best dressed woman in the country.'

Aunt Helen said she came down to visit because she had been cooking all day for the family and needed a break. Along with her husband, Aunt Helen had three line-backer sons, Jimmy, Bobby, and Billy who always kept her quite busy in the kitchen.

While leisurely walking to our house, Aunt Helen met the man we had labeled 'Black Jesus'. He quickly struck up a conversation with her and continued it until they both arrived in front of our house. At which time she was about to say goodbye when Black Jesus did a rather odd thing. . . he took Aunt Helen's right hand in his and then he kissed it! Then this person whose attire was reminiscent of the man from Galilee, casually strolled off to the store.

This was done in full view of the neighborhood, not to mention Mrs. Louise and mama who witnessed the whole thing from the porch.

Now if that wasn't enough of a shocker, Aunt Helen decides to take her place in the empty lawn chair by Mrs. Louise as though it was business as usual. Of course neither mama nor Mrs. Louise was having any of that.

"Helen, do you know that man?" Mama's voice was almost demanding.

"You don't know him? He said he had met you and two of your children." Aunt Helen had a kind of sheepish grin on her face. She knew she was trying mama's patience and she loved every second of it.

"Well, we did speak for a few minutes one day earlier this month." Mama then proceeded to relay the incident about me trying to convince Larry Wayne that the stranger was Black Jesus. Both Mrs. Louise and Aunt Helen got a kick out of that one.

"Come on Helen tell me and Gurt about that guy or I'll tell your husband that you're down here kissing strange men!" Mrs. Louise could hardly keep a straight face while sounding off that empty threat.

"He calls himself 'Solomon Seeker of Truth' although his mama named him Wilbur. . . . Wilbur Smith to be exact."

"Wilbur Smith?" Both Mrs. Louise and Mama looked at each other and started to laugh but not too loud because he might catch them as he left the store.

"He's leaving for California in about another three weeks. He's going out there to join something he calls a commune." Aunt Helen was very meticulous while recounting her most recent conversation. According to my aunt the Seeker of Truth has led a very colorful life.

"He must be one of those 'hippies'. My son says that they are all over the place." Mrs. Louise's son, Darrell, was a dentist who lived in San Francisco, California and kept her abreast of the happenings on the West Coast.

"Yeah, Walter Cronkite was talking about them once on the evening news." All those evenings of shushing us while the news was on was paying off for Mama.

Aunt Helen proceeded to give them even more information about Wilbur.

"Did you know that he has traveled to almost every state in the Union? He has worked with Civil Rights Workers in Selma and Birmingham. He was even at the March on Washington!" Mama and Mrs. Louise were completely spellbound with this new information.

"He started to dress like he does now after his first visit to California. He said that he had met a lot of people, colored and white, who he referred to as 'free thinkers' and apparently everyone dresses similar to him." Aunt Helen was enjoying being the center of attention.

"So, what's he doing here in Newport?" Mama couldn't believe anyone that worldly could find our little town interesting enough to make their home.

"Well believe it or not, that's Mrs. Sheila Thornton's nephew. His Mother, Sheila's sister, lives in Wynne. This is just one of his stops on his trip out west." Auntie really got a wealth of knowledge on that short jaunt down the street.

"How is he getting to California? Travelling is expensive. What's he doing for money?" Leave it to my mother to ask the practical questions.

"Haven't you noticed that you hardly ever see him in the morning or mid afternoon? He catches that truck on Second Street most every day.

He's chopping cotton." My aunt thought this a rather odd job for someone with the moniker 'Seeker of Truth.'

It was just about that time that the object of the ladies' 'front porch roundtable' discussion reappeared.

"Ladies, I trust that you have finished discussing the on—going comedy and sometimes tragedy which is my life." Mr. Wilbur tried to keep a serious look on his face, but it soon gave way to a very inviting smile.

Mrs. Louise spoke up first to respond to their new friend, "Oh, young man this is a small town where not much happens. You have managed to give us something very interesting to talk about."

"Yeah, VERY INTERESTING!" Aunt Helen was almost too tickled to get the words out.

With that Mr. Wilbur had to laugh himself. He then wished them all a 'good evening' and turned to make his way back to Mrs. Sheila's rented room.

After another half hour of good hearted neighborhood gossip, Mrs. Louise left in her old '56 Ford Fairlane with Aunt Helen riding shotgun.

A Lesson Taught . . . A Life Lesson Learned

We lingered outside for another thirty minutes or so until it was time to go indoors. We still had about thirty minutes before dinner, but on mama's insistence we had to come inside. I suspect the fear of a mosquito invasion was most likely the cause of our early retreat.

Charlene decided to use this time before supper to teach me how to play the card game 'spades'. I had been bugging her about this for weeks. We even convinced Daddy to join in the game when he came home from work.

Charlene was a great teacher. She covered all the basics of the game and I caught on immediately. Daddy turned out to be a very good player also. Finding this out was a bit of a shocker to both Charlene and me because we'd never seen our father play any kind of card game.

It was during this impromptu card session that my father said something to me that was so profound, that I remember it to this day.

We set up the game in our makeshift dining room. I use the term 'makeshift' because this room also served as Larry Wayne's bedroom.

It was after about ten minutes of some serious card playing and joking around that I made the fatal mistake of letting my guard down. I completely forgot that my father was sitting there with us and I said something that was completely inappropriate.

It seems that Charlene had dealt me a particularly bad hand and upon viewing the cards I shouted to her, "Girl, you be dealing some funky stuff!"

At which time my father stopped shuffling his cards and gave me a look of both intense displeasure and disappointment.

"Doris Marie, listen to the way you talk and you go to school every day!"

I was taken aback for a moment because I was sure that he was angry about the use of the word 'funky'. But the mention of the word 'school' offered up another interpretation for his obvious displeasure of my use of the English language.

Because of financial hardships my parents like some others of their generation did not finish high school. This did not diminish their great respect and admiration for educators and the institution of higher learning. Our folks (the people of our community) expected results from their children who were so privileged to attend school on a daily basis.

Evidently, my blatant misuse of the verb 'to be' with such ease and at an elevated volume did not sit well with my father. He knew that I had been taught better than that in school.

'Listen to the way you talk and you go to school every day!'

That one sentence by my father spoke volumes to me. He expected more from me. . . after all, 'I DID go to school every day.' My father expected me to demonstrate that fact not only at school, but away from school as well.

I will always remember the 'verbal spanking' I got that day. It has always inspired me to continually put forth my best effort in whatever I do.

Chapter 5

Free Show Fridays are the Best! Friday, June 30

Mama called me to the phone early Friday morning around seven-thirty. I knew it was Lillian calling to remind me about the movies. There really was no need for that, because I had been up already for an hour. It's Friday... Free Show Friday. This is the day that we could go to The Strand Theater and watch a movie for free. We lived for Free Show Fridays.

To get into the movie you had to show a ticket that you got from First National Bank or from some other cooperating business in town. This made the movie admission free, but the candy and popcorn wasn't. This is the reason why you needed to have some extra money.

Charlene and I had more than enough money. We still had some left over from mama's birthday. In 1967, you could get a carton of popcorn, a coca-cola, and a Baby Ruth for about fifty cents.

The Free show started at ten o'clock so we had plenty of time to get ready and get there. Lillian said she would ride her bike over at nine and we would go by and pick up Sheretha. We saw her yesterday after the storm and thankfully she was not on punishment and could go.

At exactly Eight fifty-five Lillian was at our front door in her favorite summer outfit. Just recently, Lillian's mom had bought her a beautiful pale blue short set from JC Penny. This was one of the outfits she usually saved for Sunday afternoons after church. I momentarily wondered why she was wearing it today. I mean we were just going to the movies.

It was Friday and Mama's last official weekday of vacation. Needless to say she offered up no arguments on our getting out of the house a bit earlier than usual. With Velma going to work and Larry Wayne tagging along with us, the house would be empty of the usual kid bickering. We all had extra money and could get lunch on our own. For the next several hours my mother would be a lady of leisure.

I can't say that either Charlene or I was particularly happy about Larry Wayne's tagging along to the movies. I CAN say that Lillian was. Larry Wayne was like the little brother she never had.

Actually he was the little brother WE never had when he was around Lillian.

Being in Lillian's presence, Larry Wayne was a different kid altogether. The truth is Larry Wayne had a little crush on Lillian. The irritating things that were reserved for Charlene and me were rarely seen by her. She got the polite 'Eddie Haskell' version whenever she was with him. Lillian babied and spoiled him to death whenever she came around to the house and Larry Wayne loved every minute of it!

We went to Calhoun Circle first to pick up Sheritha. Hopefully, she was on her best behavior and could continue on to the movies with us.

Mrs. Carmen met us at the door and we could see Sheritha peering over her shoulder. Her mom had a very pleasant look on her face which put both Charlene and me at complete ease.

"Good morning, Mrs. Carmen, can Sheritha go with us to the 'free show'?" Lillian quickly took charge and approached Sheritha's mom with the request.

"She can go, but Miss Sheritha has to complete her chores first." Mrs. Carmen took her right hand and playfully swatted Sheritha on her rear end.

"Me and Charlene are going across the street to the playground until y'all get ready, ok?" Charlene gave Larry Wayne a rather surprised look but readily went along with his idea.

I told Charlene that it wouldn't take us long to help Sheritha finish up her work and then we could go on to the movies.

"Charlene, make sure that Larry Wayne doesn't get dirty and sweaty. We're going to Ted's Lunchroom after the movies today." I tried to whisper the last part because I wanted it to be a surprise for Larry Wayne.

We tackled the breakfast dishes first. With only Sheritha and Mrs. Carmen there were very few dishes to contend with. Straitening up Sheritha's room was even easier. This came as no surprise to us, because Mrs. Carmen was adamant about keeping a clean house.

It took all of fifteen minutes to help our friend complete her chores. This included a quick inspection by her mother.

As we were leaving Sheritha's house, we motioned for Larry Wayne and Charlene to join us. She did manage to keep Larry Wayne free of dirt and grass stains from the playground.

We had ridden over to Sheritha's but decided to walk uptown to the movies. We were going to the Strand Theater and there would be no place to safely leave our bikes during the free show.

Because of the thundershower on the previous day, it was turning out to be a rather pleasant Friday. This made our trek uptown a pleasant one. Unfortunately, our extended stop at Sheritha's placed us a bit behind schedule. We had to go directly to the Strand and not make our usual stop for junk food at Sloan's Grocery. Which was a good thing because we didn't have any extra money.

When we arrived, Charlene found her buddy Barbera Carol Polson and sat with her. The balcony hadn't filled up, so we quickly found a comfortable place to sit. As a matter of fact, this was one of our favorite places to sit. . . . right there in the middle rows. From there we could easily spy on the teenagers who were making out rows below us. We could also throw the occasional popcorn kernel on the kids seated on the floor below.

We were definitely in luck today the Strand was showing JASON AND THE ARGONAUTS. Although most kids didn't find this movie scary, I was genuinely frightened by the special effects. The scene where the skeletons rise up out of the ground and then arm themselves to fight the Argonauts was really freaky!

The 'coming attractions' had finished and we were now laughing at the 'Tom and Jerry' cartoon. I decided to quickly go to the concession stand and get some much needed refreshments before the movie. Lillian and Sheritha stayed to guard our coveted spots.

I later returned armed not only with our popcorn and Pepsis, but with a bit of juicy news. Something very interesting happened at the concession stand and I was bursting at the seams to share it. As we were adjusting ourselves in our seats and getting ready for the movie, Lillian noticed how unusually fidgety I was.

"Did something happen downstairs?" I guess it didn't take a genius to read my body language.

This was just the opening I needed. I could tell Lillian about my mini adventure at the concession stand. I would have to hurry because Lillian did NOT like to talk during the movie. . . especially this movie. Sheritha was so enjoying one of her rare days of freedom that she didn't bother to turn around and give us a moment's notice.

I had just started my story when Lillian placed her index finger to her mouth and gave me the shushing sound. I had waited too long and now I've missed my opening. We would now have to wait until the end of the movie. . . dang!

Of course, we have to wait. Lillian didn't want to miss a minute of the movie. She had a real fascination with science fiction and all things Greek. She even liked those corny Hercules and Zeus cartoons that came on channel thirteen in the afternoon.

This was going to take a while too because this movie was long. After about fifteen minutes when I could no longer stand it, I gave Lillian a little nudge. I asked if I could give her a few details about my news.

"You can't tell me anything right now, Doris Marie! You know you won't be satisfied unless you can share the whole story. Now be quiet!"

Well that last 'shush' did it. I decided to sit on my news for now and lose myself in the story. This was pretty easy to do, because there were some great scenes in this movie. I could enjoy it too as long as I remembered to close my eyes during that skeleton fighting scene.

Mercifully the movie finally ended and we began to file outside. After what seemed to be an eternity, we finally moved away from the crowd outside the Strand. Charlene invited her friend Carol to join us but her mom said she had to go directly home after the movie.

We started down Walnut and headed in the direction of Front Street. Larry Wayne's friends had long since abandoned him and headed home. Fortunately, he found our company quite boring and maintained a safe distance ahead of us. Charlene and Sheritha trailed closely behind us embroiled in their own intense conversation.

"Okay, Lillian, now can I tell you what happened at the concession stand?" I could hold my excitement no longer.

"Okay, go ahead you look like you are about to burst." Lillian knew she wanted to hear about my adventure as much as I wanted to tell her about it.

"Guess who I saw in the lobby? Zach from Sloan's Grocery." Lillian's initial look of excitement soon faded from her face and gave way to serious disappointment.

"He was standing near the end of the line with two of his friends. I was getting our popcorn and drinks when I heard someone call my name." I had to continue on even though Lillian looked a bit peeved.

"This is your news? Some white boy spoke to you and now you are all excited about it! Girl, please."

I knew that Lillian didn't particularly like Zach, but she sounded almost hostile.

"Dang, Lillian. Zach's our friend. I just thought that you would get a kick out of hearing about him. But that's not all of the news."

"Keep talking and it better be good." This is the impatient side of Lillian that most people rarely saw.

I told her how Dexter White had stood and talked to me the whole time we stood in line.

"So what? Dexter White talks to everybody all the time. My mother says that he's probably going into politics one day and they have to be friendly with everybody. What's the big deal 'bout him talking to you?"

"Aw, you just jealous cause you didn't get a chance to talk to him." I still had more to tell her but I was enjoying making her agitated.

"Guess what he told me about Leonard Freeman?" A small spark of interest started to show on Lillian's face.

"You mean that boy that lives across the street from Anderson's Funeral home?" In a small town, a person's residence is usually identified by its proximity to a neighbor or a close landmark.

"Yeah Leonard. You know how he's always playing the guitar in his backyard? Well, Dexter told me that he was in a band and they were going to be on AMERICAN BANDSTAND!"

Lillian looked at me like I had just sprouted horns. "Doris Marie, I know you don't believe that. Dexter was just telling you something."

"That's what I thought at first, but Zach overheard our conversation and he knew about it too. Zach's father knows the other people in the band with Leonard." Lillian's initial look of disbelief was slowly changing.

Dexter knew of the band members through a connection at Newport High. He and another young man from the school were bike messengers for Ryan's Drugstore.

Apparently, the group was a local band out of Jonesboro. Through word-of-mouth, they must have heard of Leonard's guitar playing skills and asked him to join their group.

"Okay, Doris Marie, I can believe that Leonard is playing in some group, but American Bandstand? Come on now. What's the name of this group?"

"For your information, they're called the Garden Brothers. But now that I think about it, that American Bandstand thing does seem like a huge lie." I only said that to stop Lillian from carrying on so much. I didn't want her to ruin the memory of my time with Dexter and Zach.

By this time we had reached Ryan's Drugstore on Front Street. Ryan's was our comic book and Mad Magazine connection.

Our favorite comic books were Archie, Richie Rich and Superman. Although, I think that I was more of a fan of Superman than Lillian was. We both were crazy about Mad Magazine. It was always fun to see who or what they were making fun of in each issue.

This week they were taking on TV's I SPY or rather their version called WHY SPY? As usual it was hilarious.

We hadn't been there but for a few minutes, when in walks Zach and a few of his friends. They immediately go to the counter for sodas. Larry Wayne was already there at the counter stuffing his face with yet more food. He had already gobbled down a box of popcorn and a medium coke at the movies. Now his face was virtually being eclipsed by a large chocolate ice cream cone. That boy really does eat like Jethro. It's a good thing he had some money left over from his Kansas City trip.

During the midst of their conversation at the counter, Zach spins around and gives us a quick wave. I returned the gesture but of course Lillian purposely didn't acknowledge him. Zach then turns his attention to Larry Wayne and talks to him about the movie we'd just seen.

A few moments later he walks over and joins us at the magazine rack. He seemed to immediately turn his attention to Lillian. It was as though he wanted to finally find out for himself why she seemed to be so 'stand-offish' around him.

"Lillian, I didn't know you like Mad Magazine." Zach found a way of finally breaking the wall of silence between him and Lillian.

I guess he thought that finding out that the both of them liking the same magazine might link them together. He has clearly under estimated my friend.

"Why wouldn't I like Mad Magazine? You seem surprised by that." Lillian always had her defenses up where white people were concerned, especially if she thought her intelligence was being challenged.

"Zach, Tell Lillian about the Garden Brothers." I felt I had to quickly intercede and keep the conversation light.

"Oh, yeah you guys know Leonard Freeman. He plays in their band. My dad knows The Garden Brothers. They cut a record and Leonard is playing guitar on the record!" You could clearly see Zach's enthusiasm on the subject.

"Yeah, Yeah, Zach. Doris Marie said that you and Dexter White said that they were going to be on AMERICAN BANDSTAND. Well, are they?" Lillian questioned Zach as though he was a hostile witness in Perry Mason's courtroom.

"They actually have a record out and as far as I know, they ARE going to be on American Bandstand." Zach was desperately trying to use his most convincing voice.

"Well, I'll believe it when I see it!" It came as no surprise to me that Lillian had yet to be persuaded.

Charlene and Sheritha are still deep in their own conversation and hadn't given us a second thought. The two were pointing out the 'dirty' parts of this month's issue of TRUE CONFESSIONS. They couldn't be bothered with our childish ramblings.

While we were talking, Larry Wayne had moved on and was standing outside the store. He was still slurping down his ice cream cone which by now was mostly just cone.

Lillian, Zach, and the rest of us followed him outside still deep in our conversation. We continued our journey until we reached Ted's Lunchroom, the most popular diner in town.

We were about to enter Ted's when Zach quickly said his goodbyes and caught up to his friends. It was a moment of relief for both Lillian and me. If Zach had gone into the restaurant with us it would have made for an awkward situation. It's 1967 and Ted's like many other public places of the day, is segregated. There were no blatant signs stating the seating status. It was just understood that the 'whites' sat on one side and 'coloreds' on the other. Zach not wanting to make us (or himself) feel uncomfortable gave us a quick goodbye and decided to catch up with his friends.

Larry Wayne was the first to enter and find a table. Even though he had just gulped down a huge ice cream cone, he still had room for more.

We hadn't been seated for more than a minute when Aunt Juanita, mama's baby sister, walked over to say 'Hello.'

"Hey, Auntie! Doris Marie and Charlene are gonna buy me a Coney Island, fries and a big coke." Larry Wayne didn't get too many chances to go to Ted's and 'pig out' so he would take full advantage of this golden opportunity.

"Didn't y'all just come from the drug store? I can tell because Larry Wayne still has a little ice cream around his mouth." Aunt Juanita worked in the kitchen at Ted's. We loved running into her when we came here because she could always make us laugh.

"Hey Miss Juanita, they got you working hard today?" I'm surprised Lillian didn't call her 'Aunt Juanita' as she sometimes did.

"Hadn't been too bad today, but just wait till tomorrow. Oh Boy! Everybody and their granny always show up on a Saturday. She was right. People often went to Ted's on a Saturday after a day of shopping. It was also a place where people visiting from out-of-town frequented. Ted's had quite the reputation for being the place for a great home cooked meal.

Aunt Juanita took our order and promised to return in a few minutes. It was then that I made a startling discovery. I still had that issue of Mad Magazine I was reading from Ryans' Drugstore! I was so preoccupied with Lillian and Zach that I'd kept the magazine as I left the store.

"Why didn't y'all tell me that I had this Mad Magazine in my hand?" I whispered my complaint to the others, because I didn't want people in the restaurant (or Aunt Juania) to hear what I'd done.

"Doris Marie, I know you're not going to keep that magazine." Lillian was just trying to make me feel guilty. There's no doubt that I would return the magazine. Besides, I couldn't hide it with Larry Wayne and Charlene as witnesses. If I strolled up in my parents' house with a stolen item, that would be 'my behind.'

I didn't want to return to the drugstore for a variety of reasons; embarrassment being number two and terror as number one.

Ryan's had a rather menacing looking white woman manning the counter. She had shocking red hair which she wore in a large bouffant on top of her head. She also had a rather prominent mole that was centrally perched just above her top lip. Although she tried to hide it beneath layers of makeup, the mole was still quite visible.

I didn't have any real reason to fear this woman. Whenever I encountered her, she was cordial enough. But I always left feeling like she resented me for taking up her time.

We quickly finished off our lunch and decided to go back to Ryan's where I would pay for the magazine. This was not going to be easy. After all, I didn't know how this lady was going to react to my coming back in there. With the exception of my visits to Sloan's Grocery, I'd had few encounters with white people. The thought of going back to Ryan's frightened me. I suddenly had mental images of those students I had seen in marches and at lunch counters in Birmingham!

As we approach the store I'm feeling a little weak in the knees, but Lillian assures me that I am doing the right thing.

"Doris Marie, You have to return the magazine. We can't have 'them' thinking that we steal! It was clear that Lillian wasn't going to rest until this magazine thing was resolved.

By now, we had reached Ryan's. I gathered up my courage and approached the counter with money and magazine in hand.

"Excuse me ma'am, I mistakenly took this magazine out of the store without paying for it. I want to pay for it now." There I said it! I got the words out of my mouth without fainting!

The red haired lady had a look on her face which I found quite difficult to read. So, the next couple of sentences were something of a surprise.

"Well, Hon, there were so many kids in here I hadn't even noticed it was taken. Thank you for being such an honest and responsible young lady."

With those unexpected words, she collected my fifteen cents and gave my hand a gentle pat of approval.

Well that was easier than I thought. No racial slurs, no one was dumped with ice cream or sprayed with a water hose. The Ryan's' lady was really quite nice about the whole thing.

From that day on, a kind of mutual respect was exhibited by both the drugstore lady and me. I won't say that she was bubbling over with excitement when I came in, but there was the occasional smile and every once in a while a brief conversation.

Can We Tame a Playground Bully?

On our way home, we decided to cut through Calhoun Circle to get to Sheritha house on time. She was determined to get on her mother's good side. There were a number of fun activities going on this summer and Sheritha did not want to miss any of them. So, whenever possible she tried to go that 'extra mile' to please Miss Carmen.

After dropping off Sheritha, we quickly started off in the direction of Clay Street. We hadn't gone very far before we ran up on Emma Jean Hines who for once was not with her two troublesome friends, Verna Dean and Felicia.

"Hey, y'all been to the free show?"

What was this? Emma Jean was talking to us and being nice? She's not nice! And where were her buddies? No doubt they're off beating up some blind kid on crutches.

"Yeah, we went. Why didn't you go Emma Jean?" Lillian sounded genuinely interested.

"We got company coming for the Fourth-of-July. Mama is making all of us clean the house from top to bottom."

I guess it didn't matter that the Fourth was several days away. I guess nothing could be left to chance for a holiday that is challenging Thanksgiving for the number two spot behind Christmas.

"Where are your buddies, Verna Dean and Felicia?" I just had to ask. Those three run in a pack and it was a rare site to see any one of them alone.

"Felicia's auntie came and took her and her sister to Waukegan and Verna Dean is on punishment for the rest of the week." Emma Jean seemed to emit a sly smile when she reported the information about Verna Dean.

"Y'all wanna ride bikes up to Remmel Park?"

Well, now I've heard everything. Emma Jean Hines wants to hang out with us.

"We gotta go straight home but maybe Lillian can hang out with you." I was certain that Lillian would back out of going with some excuse.

"I'll ride bikes with you." Lillian's face showed a genuine interest. I guess Lillian had resigned herself to entertain Emma Jean since Sheritha and I were unavailable for the rest of the day.

"Okay, I'll meet you at your house. I have to go home and get permission" I never thought of Emma Jean as someone who had to get permission to do anything. The Jarretts are in for a real treat this afternoon.

"See you in about fifteen minutes." With that last exchange by Lillian, the newly formed acquaintances sped away in opposite directions.

When we got home, we found our mother digging holes for more plants. Mama grew beautiful Elephant Ears every year. The thick stalks rooted deep in the ground supported leaves that were indeed as large as the ears of an elephant!

"How was the movie? Did y'all have fun?" Mama only turned around momentarily to chat with us. She didn't want to disturb the assembly line she had going for her plants.

"It was alright. Larry Wayne can't tell you anything about it though, because him and his friends were too busy running up and down the stairs." Actually, they only went up and down the stairs about three times . . . . . I just wanted to mess with him.

This didn't bother Larry Wayne one bit. He was so full of junk food and his meal at Ted's that he headed straight for his bed to catch a nap.

As we were heading inside the house mama had some last minute instructions for us. "You girls need to unbraid your hair. I'm going to try and wash it sometime this evening or tonight."

Every other weekend without fail we had to get our hair washed and hot pressed. Of the two, the most dreaded event had to be getting my hair hot pressed. This was such a torturous procedure that it could be used in a prison war camp!

I actually didn't mind getting my hair washed. Even when the soap rushed to my tightly closed eyes, the water felt refreshing and cleansing. The difficult part came later when it was time for drying and combing the knotted tresses piled atop my head.

Mama quickly washed, dried and braided our hair. By 'our' I mean my hair and Charlene's. Velma was now at the age where she could attend to her own hair needs. Because she was working, Velma would most likely go to Miss Virginia's Beauty Shop on Front Street.

Strict instructions were given to Charlene and me to stay close to home until mama had a chance to 'straighten' our hair. Like some others of her generation, my mother hadn't quite embraced the whole natural kinky look.

It's the end of the week and there was no way mama was going to hot comb our hair tonight. She was going to be far too busy. We would most likely have to wait until Saturday evening. So, until that time we'd have to stay close to home.

It's Friday evening and Daddy just got paid. This was great news for all of us because this was also the day that Mama went grocery shopping. There was always something extra good to eat on Fridays. Extra sodas, ice cream, ham and other goodies meant that we would definitely eat well tonight and for the next couple of days.

Tonight we would have all of our favorites.

Mama will cook her famous big, fat, juicy hamburgers on white bread. Nobody and I mean NOBODY cooked better hamburgers than Gurt! She patted out thick slabs of ground beef and fried them in one of her overly used, heavy black skillets. The sliced onions that were cooked along with them gave the kitchen a mouthwatering aroma. Thick, juicy, sliced red tomatoes and pickles were the ultimate toppings for the burgers. Along with the burgers were Mama's delicious fries that were cut to near perfection and fried to a beautiful golden brown.

Mama's famously barbeque baked beans rounds out our Friday Food Fest.

The cooking was finally completed and our plates prepared. Of course, Daddy gets his food first then Larry Wayne. After which came Charlene, Velma and me. Mama as always never sat down to eat anything until all plates were filled.

Another great thing about Friday was our favorite TV show The Twilight Zone. Although it didn't happen often, mama allowed Charlene, Larry Wayne, and me to watch it in the living room while eating our supper.

Elliot came by and mama fixed him a plate. After a brief visit with mama and daddy, he and Velma joined some friends at the movies. TO SIR WITH LOVE was playing at the Strand.

About this time the phone rings and Mama answers and calls me. It was Lillian. I was glad she called but not at that time. This was a particular great episode of the Twilight Zone. A lady's face is wrapped up in bandages because of an operation she needed to change her face to 'normal'.

I take the receiver and quickly tell Lillian that I will call her right back. Thankfully, a commercial came on and I didn't miss anything. Finally, the show came back on and we resumed our nonstop gazing onto the black and white figures on the screen.

"What?" Larry Wayne was the first to voice his astonishment and disbelief on the unexpected conclusion to this story. The thing about the Twilight Zone is that you know the ending of the story is going to be strange. . . . you just don't know HOW STRANGE! This ending was THE STRANGEST!

After catching my breath and discussing the plot twists with Charlene, I gathered up my dinner plate and settled down for a nice chat with Lillian.

"Why didn't you come over to the house this evening?" Dumb question… Lillian knew that I got my hair washed every other Friday.

"You know we have to hang around the house when mama washes our hair."

"Well, you missed out on a lot of fun! Me, Sheritha, and Emma Jean rode our bikes around Calhoun Circle and out to Remmel Park."

"How did y'all get Sheritha to join you?" I knew Miss Carmen didn't really like for Sheritha to go out during the late afternoon. . . especially with someone like Emma Jean. I guess having Lillian in the group made it okay.

Lillian said Mrs. Carmen gave her the okay for Sheritha to go but told them to make sure to stay out of trouble.

I told Lillian that Mrs. Carmen probably said that last part for Emma Jean's benefit.

"Now, you know she did! She never tells "US" to stay out of trouble!" Lillian's observation had me laughing.

"What all did y'all do?" "Well, for one thing we stole some cigarettes from this lady at Remmel Park!"

"How did y'all do that? Where was the lady when the cigarettes were being taken?" I know they didn't just snatch them away from the woman.

Lillian said they took them while the lady was on the swings with her little girl. She had left her pack on a picnic table and they only took three.

"Girl, you know you telling one. You've never stolen anything in your life! Besides, what about that big lecture you gave me in Ted's today?!"

"Well, I didn't steal it!"

"Well, it must have been Emma Jean, 'cause that girl will steal ANYTHING!!"

"It wasn't Emma Jean either... It was Sheritha!"

"Ooooh Girl don't tell me Sheritha is stealing!" I moved farther into the hallway and lowered my voice. I forgot my parents were still in the kitchen.

"She just did it because Emma Jean dared her to!"

"So, what did y'all do with it?"

"We went over to the ball field by the school to smoke 'em." Lillian delivered this sentence like she was used to participating in mischievous activities.

"See now I know you're telling the biggest tale. 'Cause, you don't even know how to light a cigarette let alone smoke one."

"I didn't smoke a whole one... I just puffed and then I started to cough. Emma Jean and Sheritha smoked about a half one each and then they got to coughing too!"

"What happened to them?" I was hoping that they had hidden the cigarettes and I could join them the next time they went on a smoking adventure.

"We had to throw them away. Plus we had to get rid of the smell."

Lillian got even quieter while she spilled the beans about the rest of the afternoon. She was afraid that her parents might hear her.

"We had to go to Sloan's Grocery to buy some Juicy Fruit. We chewed about five slices each! Then we went over to Emma Jean's house and washed our hands. And even that wasn't enough so we put lotion all over our hands and arms."

"Was Zachary at the store?" I was a little miffed that Lillian was there without me. . . plus she seemed to be having all this fun while I'm sitting home with a 'nappy' head.

"Naw, Zach wasn't there, but your other boyfriend was."

"Oh God, you don't mean..."

"Yes, none other than your sweetie, Mr. Bobby Joe Walker himself." "Girl, he is so in love with you. Emma Jean asked him if y'all were getting married."

"Oh man, I don't want Emma Jean knowing my business!" I still don't like that girl.

"Girl, she was just having fun with Bobby Joe. You know she don't believe that you really like that boy."

I knew that, but Emma Jean could use this as ammunition against me if she wanted to at some future date.

"Oh yeah before I forget, ask your mama if you can spend the night at my house tomorrow night. Sheritha and Emma Jean are going to stay the night." Lillian must have forgotten that I'd just gotten my hair washed.

"Lilliian, you know I just got my hair washed and Mama probably won't get to press it until tomorrow evening."

"Well, can't you come over after she finishes it?" That cigarette must have scrambled Lillian's brain cells. She knows mama's rules when our hair has been washed

"You know mama don't like for us to go anywhere after we get our hair pressed and curled. It has to stay fresh for church."

"Oh, yeah, I forgot Mrs. Gurthalean don't want y'all sweatin' out her hard work. We'll just come over for a little while tomorrow to keep you company."

After I got off the phone with Lillian, I couldn't shake the feeling that she seemed to be having a lot more fun with her new friend Emma Jean. I immediately made the effort to dismiss that thought, remembering that Lillian and I had known each other for far too long. I really didn't see her abandoning our friendship so easily.

Besides, if she gives Emma Jean enough time, she will surely get her into some serious trouble and Lillian's parents will end that friendship with the 'quickness'!

Chapter 6

A New Kid On The Block Saturday, July 1

I woke up early Saturday morning to the sounds and smells of the grass being cut. Daddy didn't have to work on the weekends and usually spent most of Saturday doing chores in the yard. My father was a real stickler for cleanliness both inside and outside of the house.

Cutting the yard was no easy task either, considering the fact that daddy had a 'push mower'. It didn't use gas, it was strictly 'manpowered' and Butterbean was the man that powered it. Truth be told I don't think my father mind very much working outside. It gave him a chance to be alone with his thoughts and to sing selections by B.B King (which he didn't think we heard.)

Larry Wayne helped out a little, but Daddy always wound up going behind him and doing it 'his way'.

Without a doubt, daddy's other favorite outside job was washing his car. Taking out the water hose, getting a bucket from the house and gathering up old towels, detergent and polish were all a part of the car washing ritual. After all, it was well known throughout the neighborhood that Mr. Willie kept his car looking spotless. On this job, Daddy welcomed Larry Wayne's help.

While Daddy and Larry Wayne worked outside, mama got us up for breakfast and to complete our housework. We had to finish quickly because she was going to straighten Mrs. Richmond's hair that afternoon. Mrs. Richmond was Mama's supervisor on her job at the nursing home. She got her hair done by Mama every two to three weeks. Mama said she didn't mind doing it because Mrs. Richmond had a 'thin grade' of hair like Charlene and it didn't take long to press. Besides, Mama could always use the extra money.

We managed to complete our work in a rather rapid pace even if it was just Charlene and me. Velma left earlier to go to work at the hospital and had luckily avoided cleaning the house.

Mama's 'client' arrived at twelve thirty. She brought with her a jar of Royal Crown grease, a large tooth comb and her silk headscarf. After exchanging pleasantries with Charlene and me, Mrs. Richmond went to the kitchen and took her usual spot.

Mrs. Richmond informed mama that she was going to her niece's wedding on Sunday. She wanted mama to do her very best work and make her look really sharp.

Right before Mrs. Richmond arrived, mama allowed Charlene and me to pop a huge pan full of popcorn. Normally, she wouldn't have done this so early in the day especially with her company coming. But mama wanted to pacify us because we couldn't go outside until our hair had been pressed.

We didn't mind not going outside this afternoon. They would be showing Shirley Temple Movies on Channel three and we didn't want to miss it. We loved those movies, especially the one where she searches for her father whom she was told had died in the Boer War.

Another reason staying in wasn't so bad today was that the temperature had started to climb. Although it had been somewhat pleasant this morning, the temperature had risen at least five degrees by one o'clock. There was no way we could have gone outside today even if we wanted to do so. The heat would make us sweat too much causing mama to have to wash our hair again and nobody wanted that.

About fifteen minutes on the heels of Mrs. Richmond's arrival came Sheritha, Lillian, and Emma Jean. I was afraid that mama might make us all go to my room. As a rule of thumb, we weren't allowed to have our company in the living room. . . especially if we were eating. Either mama was too busy tending to her client or she was putting her total trust in Charlene and me to monitor the situation, but she didn't say anything to us.

Fortunately, Lillian and Sheritha were familiar with mama's living room rules. Emma Jean followed their lead and respectfully placed her glass of lemonade on the floor, while eating the popcorn we'd offered all of them earlier.

We were all so engrossed in our Saturday afternoon movie feature that conversation had all but come to a complete stand still. Mama even came up to the living room a few times because as she put it, "Y'all are too quiet. . . . you must be up to something."

After seeing that we were indeed okay and not up to anything, mama retreated back to the kitchen. She was almost finished with Mrs. Richmond's press, curl, and 'gossip' session.

Then out of the blue came an unexpected revelation from Emma Jean.

"My Mama said that I could have Shirley Temple curls to go with my new Fourth of July outfit."

Looks of amazement shot across the room. Emma Jean's desire to wear her hair similar to that of the prissiest (and not to mention the whitest) girl in Hollywood was shocking to say the least.

Emma Jean wasn't exactly a 'Shirley Temple' kind of girl.

I guess Emma Jean's relationship with Lillian had put her at ease enough within her new surroundings that she felt she could share this bit of information with us.

"What you getting curls for on the Fourth? You just gonna sweat it out before the day is over." I don't know why I lashed out at her like that. But Shirley Temple curls? Watching Shirley Temple was one thing, but wanting to look like her was quite another.

"You know what? I think I'll get some too, Emma Jean." Lillian chimed in quickly after seeing the look of embarrassment on Emma Jean's face.

"Well, the two of you can go right ahead, with your head full of Shirley Temple curls. It is gonna be ninety degrees on the Fourth and those curls are not going to hold up." Thank God, for Sheritha's voice of support.

Although, I did secretly wonder if Sheritha was more jealous of the girls' ability to wear the hair style than how the heat would affect it.

Emma Jean and Lillian both had what we use to refer to as 'good hair'. Either could easily pull off wearing those junior Hollywood curls. Sheritha on the other hand had rather short hair. It couldn't begin to dangle freely from her scalp in a Shirley Temple fashion.

"Emma Jean, my mama will press and curl your hair when you come over this evening to spend the night."

I guess Lillian was still trying to make Emma Jean feel at ease after the cutting remarks by both Sheritha and myself.

With both Sheritha and Emma Jean spending the night, I was once again feeling left out. That was until I learned of a change of plans in tonight's sleepover lineup.

Sheritha had agreed earlier to the sleepover but had to back out. She thought she had company from Detroit coming in this weekend. We find out later that the company was her father coming from Chicago. Mrs. Carmen hadn't told Sheritha because she wanted to surprise her.

"Remember I did ask you last night over the phone, Doris Marie. You said you had to get your hair pressed this evening, otherwise you could join us." Once again Lillian interjects words of solace so I wouldn't feel so 'left-out.'

"So, what are y'all gonna do tonight?" I had to know just how Lillian planned to entertain this wild child.

"Most of the time we'll probably be getting our hair done. We won't be able to do anything after that except watch TV and listen to records."

Emma Jean didn't respond to Lillian, but instead gave her a look of complete agreement. If they were going to do all of that with their hair it was surely going to be a long night.

Having Emma Jean over was going to be a new adventure for the Jarrett clan. I wonder if she will like Lillian's Beatles and Rascals' records.

Maybe she'll convince Lillian to help her beat up a few kindergarteners on their way home!

Emma Jean and company departed soon after the end of the movie. After which Charlene and I quickly cleaned up the little popcorn debris left by the girls. At first Charlene was not going to help me, reminding me that they were 'my' friends and not hers. She quickly changed her mind when she remembered that Mama would also hold her responsible for the condition of the living room.

A Fiery Hot Metal Comb Being Raked Through Your Scalp!

Daddy hated the smell of burning hair. This was most likely the reason why he chose to be outside for most of today.

After cutting the yard and washing the car, Daddy and Larry Wayne went fishing at Newport Lake. When they arrived later that evening with their cache of buffalo and catfish, Larry Wayne couldn't wait to tell mama about the water moccasin that he and daddy encountered while fishing.

Mama tried to get him to quiet down, but Larry Wayne kept babbling on without an end in sight.

He knew like we all did that mama had an almost paralyzing fear of water moccasins. Snakes in general frightened her, because as mama put it, she had seen enough of them while growing up in the country. Water Moccasins were different though. To my mother they were more sinister than the occasional garden or chicken snake found by anyone who lived in rural areas.

Mama finally quieted Larry Wayne's never ending ghoulish details about the snake he'd seen. She then ushered him and daddy outside to clean their stinky but delicious catch of the day.

Meanwhile, Charlene and I were told to take down our hair and get it ready to be pressed. Mama probably wouldn't get to it until later this evening.

Supper came and went without much fanfare. The fried fish, smothered potatoes, and slaw with raisins were quickly eaten.

After such a delicious meal, Charlene and I quickly cleared the kitchen without any prompting from mama. We didn't mind doing it because mama had been on her feet all day and could use the break. It was about this time that Mrs. Louise came down for a short visit. She and Mama sat on the porch relaxing with chilled glasses of Lipton tea with lemons. Mrs. Louise was filled to the brim with information about all the out-of-towners she had run into today. Most were here for the big wedding at First Baptist Church on Sunday and others for the Fourth holiday.

While Mama was winding up her visit with Mrs. Louise, Charlene and I finished cleaning the kitchen. Cleaning the kitchen was generally a pretty boring job. You wash the dish. . . . .you dry the dish. You wash the dish. . . . you dry the dish. Thankfully, there was the radio to help liven up the chore.

WDIA had completely slipped away so we found that station out of Nashville that we sometimes listened to when in a pinch. It was mostly a Blues station, but it did play some Motown tunes. Aretha

Franklin's RESPECT was being played and of course Charlene had to sing along as only she could.

By the time Mama came in from the front porch, we had cleared the kitchen of all sights and smells of the recent meal. She immediately made a beeline for the drawer that held her 'hot' combs and curlers.

In an unusual turn of events, mama decided to place me in the 'hot seat' first. This was not the normal order for pressing hair. The general order is oldest to youngest, in which case Charlene would go first.

It was a well known fact that between Charlene and me, my hair was a bit longer and far thicker than hers. The thickness of my tresses made pressing my hair a monumental task. This is the reason why I guess mama decided to tackle my head first just to get it over with quickly.

"Come on Doris Marie! Let me get this wild head done first. Make sure you bring a towel and the Royal Crown grease from the bathroom."

Man I hated getting my hair pressed. The curling part was okay, but pressing took a long, long time. And It could be dangerous.... well, maybe not dangerous, but it did hurt.

Just picture it. A fiery hot, metal comb is being raked through your hair and across your scalp.....repeatedly!

First, Mama parts, combs, and greases the individual sections of my hair. Then she lifts the heated comb from the stove and waves it briefly in the air right before pulling it through the sectioned strands held in her left hand.

I could just feel the heat from the hot comb as it comes in contact with my scalp. You try to sit as motionless as possible. Any movement could mean certain death!

Well, maybe 'certain death' is a bit of an exaggeration. You were more likely to get a little nick of a burn to your ear!

Even though getting your hair pressed was a slow process, Mama could make it a lot of fun by telling stories about her and Aunt Helen when they were kids.

One story told of how Aunt Helen protected mama from two Polish boys they had to encounter on a daily basis as they walked to school. It seems that these young men would tease and taunt them every day. One day the teasing went too far and one of the boys threw a rock and hit my mother. This was too much for Aunt Helen who chased the boy down and beat him up!

Mama always ended any story involving Auntie by saying "You know Helen was never scared of anybody!"

But there were times that Mama could take out a little revenge against us while we were in her 'chair'. It involved our 'edges' and/or the 'kitchen' portions of our hair. She always got me when pressing the edges near my ears. This is the place where she might say something like:

"Remember, when you talked back to me last Thursday? Now hold your ear down."

"Okay now, bend your head down so I can get your kitchen. Uh, did I hear you use a bad word to your little brother this morning?"

HELP ME LORD JESUS!

These were literally moments of terror for those of us who had to go under Gurt's hot comb. She wouldn't burn you. . . . well, not on purpose anyway. But, she would scare the life out of you because she could make you THINK she was going to burn you!

It didn't take too long for mama to finish. After polishing off the thick, mangled mess on my head, Mama usually pressed Charlene's hair in record time.

Having finished the 'press and curl' session, we were given strict instructions to carefully tie up our heads AND NOT GET IT WET WHILE BATHING!!

Fortunately, it wasn't too hot tonight especially with the window fans going full blast.

I graciously let Charlene go first in the bathroom because I had other plans. Tonight was movie night.

The Brand New Kid On The Block

Saturday night was a great night because Channel 4 out of Little Rock showed 'Saturday Night at the Movies.' Some of Hollywood's best was shown on that night and I had a front row seat to watch them all on our old black and white set.

I know it sounds very much like a cliché, but the movies definitely had a way of transporting me to another time and place.

This is where I saw Burt Lancaster shake the revival tent rafters and save souls in Elmer Gantry. I was mesmerized by Robert Duvall's portrayal of the mute Boo Radley as he rescued Scout and Jem in To Kill a Mockingbird. The great Sidney Poitier held me spellbound as he and his family saw certain freedom with the arrival of an insurance check.

Tonight my favorite Betty Davis movie was showing. What Ever Happened to Baby Jane was both scary and funny. The part where Baby Jane serves up a rat to her sister (played by Joan Crawford) always frightened me then made me almost wet my pants from laughing so hard.

The movie hadn't been on but for a few minutes when all of a sudden I heard someone rushing onto our front porch. It was Mr. Glen Lansky who lived in the double tenant house across the street.

Glen was a tall, stocky built man with thick black hair and large brown eyes. I had such a crush on him. This feeling was continually reinforced whenever Mr. Glen greeted me with his usual salutation of "Hey Baby Girl!" Every time he spoke to me I could see his every word in neon lights.

Mrs. Gail was a petite lady who by now was in her ninth month of pregnancy. She had what mama called a cute little 'baby bump.' She always wore her hair in a neck-length bob and dressed in the cutest maternity outfits.

"Mr. Willie! Mr. Willie!" Recognizing the voice heard sailing through the night air, I started for the porch. My efforts however were thwarted by mama rushing to the front room while reminding me about opening the door at night.

Mama and Mr. Glen spoke for less than a minute before she came running back inside to wake daddy. Glen quickly rescues Mrs. Gail from the sidewalk and leads her to the green and white slide swing on our front porch.

"Willie, wake up! Gail is having the baby and Glen's car won't start! They need us to drive them to Newport Hospital!"

"Huh? What's all that noise?" It seems that Daddy was pretty wiped out from all the yard work and fishing he'd done today. Waking him up from a sound sleep was gonna take a minute or two.

Finally Mama rouses Daddy out of his deep sleep. She filled him in on Glen and Gail's dilemma while helping him to quickly dress.

After daddy gets a cool glass of water to drink and splashes a bit on his face, he was ready to go. Within a matter of minutes the youngest residents of Clay Street were on their way to bringing a new life into the world.

Before leaving, mama rushed through the standard 'house rules'. Charlene being in charge was a given since she was older. We knew to keep our doors locked until Velma came home or Mama and Daddy returned from the hospital. We also knew to call Aunt Helen in case of emergency. Fortunately, Larry Wayne was knocked out from today's activities. Once he went to sleep he was in a near comatose state. So, he was unaware of all that was happening right there under his nose.

It was really too bad he missed seeing Gail. Even though she was in a lot of pain, she was still strikingly beautiful. She must have anticipated her coming attraction because she had Mama to straighten and curl her hair just last week. Mama said mothers (especially new ones) like to look pretty when giving birth.

Gail had on her prettiest maternity outfit. It was an attractive two piece pink skirt set. The top was pink and white polka dots while the skirt was a solid soft pink. Glen had given her a beautiful baby pin that she wore on the outfit's white collar. The pin was of a beautiful little black girl and boy, which he had bought in Memphis.

Mama going to the hospital to bring home a baby brought back fun memories for Charlene and me. When Mama was in the hospital having Larry Wayne, she left Velma in charge. She did a pretty good job keeping the house clean and our hair combed. She even ironed Daddy's work clothes to his satisfaction. But the one thing she couldn't quite handle was the cooking. She burned almost everything! On the plus side Daddy was forced to take us all out to eat at Ted's Lunch Room at least twice.

It had only been a few minutes since Mama and Daddy left and already the house was starting to get a little creepy. It's always strange the way a house emits noises when your parents are away. In an effort to make it a little less scary, Charlene turned on all the lights.

We found the flashlight and got Larry Wayne's baseball bat and headed for the living room to watch TV with a feeling of safety. After a few minutes of feeling comfortable, Charlene and I ventured off to the kitchen to get some ice cream. We had just filled our bowls with

*the creamy delights (strawberry for Charlene and chocolate for me)
when we heard people talking. As we tip toed toward the front we
were relieved to find out it was just Velma and Elliot.*

*Dang! She would show up now! Just when we were about to
enjoy an illegal night time treat. Velma was sure to put a stop to our
fun and make us go to bed. Dang!*

*We took our chances and proceeded on to enjoy our ice cream.
Maybe Velma wouldn't be too mean if Elliot was with her.*

*We were still watching the 'Baby Jane' movie and my favorite
scene was coming up when Elliot and Velma decided to come in from
the sidewalk. Apparently they were taking advantage of what they
thought was Daddy's generosity in letting them "visit" for a few extra
minutes.*

*"Elliot, I have to get inside before Daddy comes out here and runs
you off!" Velma manages to break away from Elliot's embrace long
enough to come into the living room. Meanwhile Elliot is screaming
his "goodnights" to Mama and Daddy as Velma is apologizing for
coming in so late.*

*"Uh, I don't know who y'all talking to.....Mama and Daddy are
at the hospital!" Charlene loved delivering this message.*

*"What happened? Is Mama okay?" Velma went immediately to
panic mode with the thought of our mother being ill.*

*"Nah, don't get all upset. Ain't nobody sick. They had to take
Glen and Gail to the hospital. Mrs. Gail is having the baby and Mr.
Glen's car wouldn't start." Charlene continued with her explanation
of our parents' absence.*

*"So, basically what you're saying is that Mama and Daddy aren't
here and I could have stayed out a little later. They never would have
known anything about it. Dang!"*

*She sure recovered from Mama's imagined sickness pretty quick.
But she couldn't be more wrong about that 'staying out later' thing.
Our sister Charlene had a mouth as big as Texas and she would have
spilled the beans about Velma staying out late. And if she forgot, I
was ready to sing like a canary.*

*"Well, y'all are just living it up while Willie and Gurt are away.
Maybe I should get Larry Wayne up so he can join in the festivities."*

Now that was an empty threat. My sister wasn't about to awaken our little brother out of a sound sleep. He would be ten different kinds of cranky and hungry to boot!

The movie ended and we were watching the news when we heard our parents at the back door. Mama was all smiles when she told us about her evening. She had planned to come right back, but Mrs. Gail was scared and begged her to stay longer. Even with all of Daddy's protests, Mama managed to convince him to stay. It was a good thing too, because Mr. Glen was as nervous as a cat! He needed someone there to talk him through it.

Gail had a beautiful baby girl who she named Camille Antoinette. I thought that it was such an exotic name and not particularly southern at all especially her middle name, Antoinette.

Mama said that baby Camille had big brown eyes and a head full of curly black hair that was beautifully matted around her forehead. Mr. Glen couldn't resist placing her tiny little fingers and toes in his mouth that is when he got up enough courage to actually hold her.

I could hardly wait for the little family to return across the street with their brand new addition.

CHAPTER 7

The Halleluiah Place Sunday, July2

Sundays were always a bit hectic around our house. After all we had only the one bathroom and six people using it to get ready for church. Mama and daddy weren't the problem because they got up at the 'crack of dawn' and easily cleared the bathroom. Larry Wayne generally zipped in and out to only as mama would say, 'glance at the water' and would almost meet himself leaving!

That would leave my sisters and me. Now on regular weekday bathroom visits, we'd stroll in when it was free. On Sundays however, it was always a race for the bathroom door. Mostly, we were trying to beat Velma. It was a known fact that teenage girls could spend an eternity in the bathroom and our oldest sister was no exception to that rule.

Getting her hair to look 'just right' and putting on just the hint of makeup took Velma about forty minutes every Sunday. This caused Charlene and me to quickly bathe and dress for church so that we wouldn't be late for Sunday school.

Once dressed and prepared for church with Bibles, Sunday purses, hankies, and fifty cents for Offering, we made a swift start for the 'Halleluah Place.' Halleluah Place was the colorful name given to our church by our little baby cousin Braden.

Once again we were using the car services of Laura Marks, Velma's best friend. On cool pleasant days or slightly warm days, Charlene, Larry Wayne and I would opt to walk. But on particularly hot days or days with frigid temps, we'd take advantage of the ride with Velma and Laura. Because we wanted to stay as fresh as possible for church, we took advantage of Laura's car.

Our church was Morning Star Baptist Church located on Vine Street which was several blocks from our house. There was a time I wished we lived on Vine because I saw a certain prestige associated with living on the same street as a church.

Our pastoral leader was Reverend Samuel Hezikiah Fitzhugh. Reverend Fitzhugh was a short, stocky, baldheaded man in his mid sixties. It was always a source of amusement to watch him wipe the tiny beads of sweat during his sermon. This process was generally the same each time; removal of glasses, wipe neck, top of his head and finish up with mopping every crevice of the face.

Every Sunday Pastor Fitzhugh would give the most fiery speeches about the evils and consequences of sin all of which frightened me terribly. On more than one occasion, I've awaken suddenly from a night's sleep after picturing myself struggling to fend off demons from the bowels of Hell!

While Velma and Laura ushered Larry Wayne off to Miss Betty's class, Charlene and I found seats in the choir stand. Our church was rather small so Sunday school classes were sectioned off to different areas of the sanctuary. The adults and teenagers met in the Fellowship Hall, pre-teens in the choir stand, and all kids nine years old and under met in the back pews.

"Good morning, girls. You just made it in time we haven't quite started yet."

"Good Morning, Mrs. Macdonald." Charlene and I chimed in our greetings in virtual perfect sync.

Mrs. Lacy Macdonald was a short, mocha skinned woman with short, black, hair that she kept cut and very neatly styled. Not only was she beautiful, but she was without a doubt one of the most pleasant people you'd ever want to meet. She made sure that we had fun while learning our Bible lessons.

Mrs. Macdonald was also the 12th grade English Literature teacher at WF Branch. Although quite petite in stature, she was known to be a stern taskmaster who would go 'toe-to-toe' with anyone.

Of course it didn't hurt any that Mrs. Lacy was married to Ray Macdonald, the boys' PE and basketball coach. Mr. Macdonald was a tall and quite muscular built, ebony-skinned man who rarely smiled. He had such a menacing presence that he could silence an entire group of rowdy students just by entering a room.

We were nearing the end of our lesson and I was starting to feel a bit uneasy. To keep us involved, Mrs. Macdonald usually engaged us in a discussion of the lesson's objective to see if we could relate it to a real world experience. I didn't mind this part at all. It was the next part that was making me nervous as a cat.

Mrs. Macdonald would choose one of us to say a prayer at the end of the lesson. You never knew WHO she was going to choose, so you had to be prepared. My problem was that I sometimes got the 23rd Psalm and the Lord's Prayer a bit mixed up. I knew them both, but I would sometime forget which prayer went with which title.

Fortunately, if called upon today I was well prepared. I had the title and first line of The Lord's Prayer in my left hand. I also had the title and first line of The 23rd Psalm in my right hand.

The lesson ended and just as I had feared, Mrs. Lacy called my name for prayer. As luck would have it, Mrs. Lacy switched things up a bit this week. As opposed to having someone come before the class to lead the prayer, she had us to immediately hold hands. She then asked me to lead the 23rd Psalm.

This almost derailed me, but I had just enough time to quickly view my right hand to scan the first few lines of The 23rd Psalm. Thank God!(literally) This was the one that I was most familiar.

As we left, Mrs. Lacy gathered us into a group hug while uttering her usual statement of departure:

"I love you much... now go and conquer the world!"

It was about 10:15 and church services starts at 10:30. We have about ten 'good' minutes before we have to start filing back inside. Charlene abandoned me for her friends. Velma and Larry Wayne accompanied Laura home to pick up her mother. Her father was feeling a bit under the weather and was staying home today.

Suddenly, I felt a thumping on my right ear lobe. It was my cousin Bobby playing his favorite game of sneaking up behind me to thump my ear then look away like nothing happened. I hated that. It was ten different kinds of annoying.

"Stop it, Bobby! You play too much!" I wasn't really that annoyed with him. Don't get me wrong I did hate having my ear thumped, but he never did it in a mean way and he did know when to stop.

"Stop it, Bobby you play too much!" That was the other annoying thing he did.... repeating what I'd just said in a really irritating, nasal voice. He then proceeded to thump me yet again.

That was a huge mistake on his part. I then turned and kicked him in the shin. Not enough to leave a bruise, but just enough to make him grimace in pain.

"Okay, okay I'm sorry cuz. Dang it girl you play rough!"

He wasn't that hurt. I think he apologized just so I'd feel a sense of victory in our very minor skirmish.

"Y'all going to the big wedding this afternoon at First Baptist?" Bobby knew the answer to that question. The bride in question was the niece of mama's boss.

I told him how mama had not only pressed our hair but had taken care of Mrs. Richmond too in preparation for the wedding.

"There's a good chance that mama might not be in church this morning, 'cause I know she's tired from pressing all those heads yesterday!"

"Didn't Mrs. Gail have her baby last night?" I had barely finished my sentence before Bobby burst in with that question... another one of which I'm certain he knew the answer.

"Yeah, mama and daddy had to take them to the hospital because Mr. Glen's car wouldn't start."

Bobby gave a little chuckle at this point.

"Now Mr. Glen knows he should get rid of that car it's always stopping on him."

"I know that's right. It's a good thing that Mr. Glen needed daddy for something as important as going to the hospital. Otherwise, Daddy would never have gotten out of his bed."

About this time Laura and Velma pulled up with Mrs. Nora, Laura's mother, who was seated in the front seat. She was dressed in a beautiful cap-sleeved yellow dress with a soft, floral pattern. She wasn't wearing a hat which was quite unusual for Mrs. Nora. She did have several small artificial sunflowers embedded in her tightly curled black hair. They were carefully pinned on the left side of her head.

"Hey, Mrs. Nora, I like your dress."

"Well, Hey there, Doris Marie! How are you this fine morning?!"

"I'm good and how are you this morning?" People always say the same thing when greeting each other. You ask how someone is doing and the answer is generally the same.

"Well, Baby Girl I thank GOD that I am doing VERY WELL this morning.

With that brief exchange of pleasantries Mrs. Nora joined Laura and Velma who were a few steps ahead of her.

I was waiting for mama and daddy to arrive but it appeared that they were going to be a little late getting here. I immediately looked around for Larry Wayne who was chasing after one of his friends.

"Larry Wayne get your little square behind over here!"

"I'm waiting on Mama."

That boy will use any excuse to play.

"No, you come on right now. Mama and daddy are running late and they might not come at all."

"Okay, Okay." Larry Wayne knew from past experiences not to argue with me because he would lose.

Now finding a place to sit in church could be a 'tricky' situation.

The ideal place to sit would be the middle or back pews. These areas were less active than the front rows.

Old people usually sat up front and sitting beside them could be dangerous. It was especially hazardous sitting by old ladies who had a tendency to 'get happy' and 'shout'.

When an old lady gets to shouting she was subject to lose all control. This spirit filled behavior might result in her arms, legs, and wig being sent into three different directions!

The scariest place of all to sit was beside Mrs. Bernetha Stallworth. Mrs. Bernetha was a businesswoman who sold insurance. We lived beside her on Front Street for years before moving onto Clay. She was a well dressed lady in her mid to late fifties. Mrs. Bernetha was one of a few ladies who still wore those stockings with the seam in the back.

It wasn't her shouting that frightened me. Mrs. Bernetha rarely shouted and when she did it was pretty low key. It was actually something that she wore which on more than one occasion gave me nightmares.

Mrs. Bernetha was the proud owner of a 'fox wrap.' This was quite a 'find' for women in the 1960s and especially for a black woman.

But that wrap frightened me. It was like an actual fox pelt. It had the fox tail, feet, and face which included the little fox beady eyes.

Sitting beside Mrs. Bernetha while she was wearing that fox wrap could be terrifying. I always had the feeling that her wrap was about to pounce right on me!

Great! There were available spaces beside Laura and Velma in the pews on the right. Mrs. Nora had moved to the front and she was sitting by Mrs. Bernetha. (Good luck Mrs. Nora!)

Charlene sat in the back with her classmate Barbara Carol Colson.

The church began to fill up rather quickly and with a few more people than usual. This was due partly because this was the First Sunday and also because of the big wedding this afternoon. The latter bringing in a few new faces from out of town.

Soon after Larry Wayne and I were seated, an attractive family sat on the bench in front of us. Normally, that wouldn't have bothered me, but the wife was wearing a rather large hat. It was navy blue and white with a wide brim that blocked my view of the choir stand.

This hat was really going to pose a problem. For me, the best part of church was seeing and listening to the gospel choir.

Now, I don't want to take anything away from Rev. Fitzhugh's sermon. He could really stir up a crowd and bring people to a fever pitch. But the choir led by Mrs. Izetta Kilburn's high soprano voice singing "It's Amazing" brought the congregation to their feet!

While trying to look around the newcomer's hat, I noticed she had a young daughter and son about my age. Like the mother, the daughter was very well dressed. She also wore a navy blue and white hat although nowhere near as elaborate as her mother's.

The daughter donned a small white purse with matching gloves and shoes. She wore a slim fitting dark blue dress with cap sleeves and a small white bow at the waist. If she was this dressed up for our service, I can't wait to see how she will be dressed for the wedding!

We'd only been seated for a few minutes when the Deacons approached the altar. It was time to pray and start the service.

"I LOVE THE LORD, HE HEARD MY CRY"

"I.I lo. . . . ve the.aah Lord, Heeee heard my . . . e. . . I. . . I cry"

"AND PITIED EVERY GROAN LONG AS I LIVE"

"And pit. . . . ed e. . . . .very groa. . . n lo. . . ng aeh. . . .asss I . . . I live

"AND TROUBLES RISE, I HASTEN TO HIS THRONE"

"A.nd trou. . . . bles ri. . . .ise, I ha.aasten to.ooo hi. . . . isss thro. . . .ne"

This was always a kind of sad part of the service for me. It wasn't so much the words (although they were sad enough) it had to be the way it was sung by the Deacons. It was a very slow and sluggish type song with words that were difficult to decipher. It didn't matter much anyway, because most people hummed their way through the whole thing.

When the deacons finished, I spotted an unfamiliar couple inching their way in the back trying very hard not to be noticed. It was always a little embarrassing when you arrived late for church. As soon as you come in practically everyone turns around all at once to see who it is.

Before the sermon got underway, Rev. Fitzhugh acknowledged the visitors and asked them to stand. Several families stood and pretty much said the same thing:

"Giving honor to God who is the head of my life, we are The Williamson family from Detroit, Michigan. We bring you greetings from New Light Missionary Baptist Church where the Reverend Doctor Jesse L. McKeon is the Pastor."

I learned that the family seated in front of us was from Little Rock. Their last name was Richmond and they were here for the big wedding this afternoon. Unlike the other visiting families, Mrs. Richmond took the time to introduce each member of her clan. I noticed some of the congregation looking at each other with a slight smile while she spoke, because she seemed to do so in a kind of "proper English" way. Speaking the 'King's English' correctly was not frowned upon, but 'masking' her southern accent was a major mistake.

Nothing irritated church folk more than someone speaking in a way that suggests that they were 'putting on airs.' This was especially true if the person in question had roots in the South.

(It was later revealed that Mr. and Mrs. Richmond were originally from Marianna, Arkansas.)

I learned the names of the two kids seated in front of us after Mrs. Richmond revealed them during her lengthy introduction. The girl, Diane and the boy, Woodrow stood alongside their parents in a very dignified manner.

The boy's curly, black hair looked freshly cut. He wasn't as dressed up as his mom and sister. As a matter of fact he had on a pair of jeans paired with his short-sleeved white shirt. Wearing jeans were almost unheard of at our church. I mean if you were going to choir practice or Vacation Bible school you could get by with wearing jeans or even a shorts set. Donning jeans during Sunday church services might solicit disapproving looks from the church ladies.

"We want to thank the Richmond Family and all the other visitors who are worshipping with us this morning. Man, I tell you this is gonna be some kinda fancy wedding this afternoon. If the hotels would let us in, the white folks would be making some BIG money this weekend!"

"There were so many colored folks in Ted's Lunchroom yesterday that my wife and I couldn't find a table. We wound up sitting at the counter on the white side. You know Mr. Ted has always been a decent man plus he wasn't about to turn down that money!"

Reverend Fitzhugh was never at a loss for words. As Aunt Helen might say, "What comes up comes out!"

We had a very lively, spirited service that morning. The choir had everyone on their feet several times while singing hymns like 'It's Amazing' and 'Jesus is on the Main Line.' Reverend Fitzhugh continued to rally the parishioners with his fiery sermon while stopping periodically to mop the sweat from his face.

Services ended at around twelve-thirty at which time the second (unofficial) part of Fellowship starts. This is a great time for members of the congregation to engage in a little neighborly, Christian chit-chat.

This practice was done more in depth by the women than by the men. A few handshakes and "How you doin' Doc?" by the husbands and they were pretty much out the door.

The women, however, had to spend ample time getting caught up in the lives of their church sisters:

"How's your mama doing?"

"Y'all going to Chicago this summer?"

"They tell me your boy is headed for the army, well maybe he'll get lucky and they won't send him over there."

"I hear Mrs. Marlene is pretty low sick, have you been by to see her?"

"No, I hadn't heard about Sister Marlene. Well bless her heart. If you see her before I do, give her my best and I will come and sit with her real soon."

"Girl, I heard that the folks at Mount Moriah are trying to get rid of Pastor Ellis ain't that something? Lord have mercy, colored folks just won't do!"

This exchange could go on for some time. But irritated husbands and starving children always caused these meetings to come to a halt. One by one each of the church sisters had to leave their conversation on the urgency of a very needy family member. At which time they would be escorted home to serve up the traditional Sunday dinner (which they had slaved over the night before!)

On the plus side, the huge meal paired with the Reverend's sermon was better than a sleeping pill. It was subject to put everyone out cold and mothers everywhere would at long last have some peace and quiet.

Charlene and I elected to walk home after church while Larry Wayne decided to ride back with Velma and Laura. He said it was because of the heat, but it was really because he knew they would be stopping at Dairy Queen for ice cream.

The walk down Vine Street was quite pleasant. Even though the temperature was noticeably warm, it wasn't sticky hot. I was having a rather difficult time keeping up with Charlene. The heat always accelerated her pace which caused me to speed up my steps.

"What's the hurry? There will be plenty of fudge bars by the time we get there!" Although I knew it wouldn't work, I was trying to get my sister to slow it down a bit. If I walked too fast I was subject to work up a sweat.

"The last time we were late getting to the store, Mr. Sloan had run out of fudge bars." Charlene had no intention of missing out on those chocolate treats.

Fudge bars and sip dips were favorites on a hot summer day. And since Mrs. McDaniel's store wasn't open on a Sunday (our sip-dip connection) we had to rely on Mr. Sloan's grocery for our cool treats.

"Charlene, will you slow down already! If we get too hot we will sweat out our hair and you know Mama will be mad about that." I thought a little "mama" fear would help her to change to a more leisurely stride.

"Girl, will you stop whining besides we're almost there!"

True we were almost there as a matter of fact we arrived just moments later. My concern now was the two blocks we had to walk to get home.

"Can I help you, girls?" Mr. Sloan had positioned himself behind the counter as though he was getting ready for a large crowd.

Mr. Sloan's store was only open for business a short time on Sundays, between the hours of 12:30 pm and 3pm. This time captured that last minute shopper for Sunday Dinner and it serviced the "after church" kid crowd.

The "after church" kid crowd could be a sizeable one. It was comprised of that group of teens and preteens who had held back change from the collection so they could purchase candy, chips, cookies, or pop from the store.

Going to Mr. Sloan's after church was not a practice Charlene and I could participate in very often. When Daddy gave us money for church he expected for us to put ALL of it into that collection plate. So, any money we spent there was money we had hidden from our parents.

Plus Mama did not want us to waste anything on our church clothes. Our stopping to eat a fudge bar on a hot summer day wasn't very smart. It would take some very creative moves on our part to avoid spilling the melted remnants onto our clothes.

There were only a handful of kids and several adults in Mr. Sloan's store when we arrived.

Just like my sister and I, most of these kids were dressed in their Sunday best and were spending part of the money they'd be given for the collection plate. There were also a small group of kids who were wearing street clothes and obviously hadn't attended church that day.

We were surprised to see Mr. George and Mrs. Bessie Cross. They were an elderly couple who had been our neighbors when we lived on Front Street. I rarely saw them since we moved and to see them on a Sunday was even rarer since they attended First Baptist.

Apparently, Mr. George had forgotten to pick up the lemons and sugar needed for their iced tea which would accompany their Sunday dinner.

I along with everyone else in the store learned of Mr. George's colossal mistake because Mrs. Bessie proceeded to tell Mr. Sloan all about it. This tickled Mr. Sloan to no end.

"All I asked Husband to do on yesterday was to pick up these few items at the store." They often referred to each other as "Husband" and "Wife."

"Oh, now Wife hush your complaining! We got our groceries and you even got your snuff and tobacco, so get your parasol ready for the walk home."

Mr. George was really teasing Mrs. Bessie now, he knew she didn't like for folks to know about her snuff and tobacco cravings.

Mrs. Bessie hands him the packages and then pretends to slightly hit him with her umbrella.

Mr. Sloan stops his laughter long enough to inquire about their transportation. Since he saw Mrs. Bessie holding her parasol, he wondered if they were riding or walking. He was about to offer up a ride home when Mr. George assured him that they would be alright and Mr. Sloan shouldn't bother himself.

Mr. Sloan quickly reassured him that this would not be a bother at all and quickly ushered them outside to his car leaving his wife and Zach in charge of the store.

Actually, Mr. George had a car. It was a 1947 Nash Sedan, which he babied like the child he and Mrs. Bessie never had. Unfortunately, the car conked out on them earlier that day right before church started. This prompted them to set out on foot for morning services.

Mr. Sloan had an ulterior motive for being so gracious in volunteering his chauffeuring services to the elderly couple. He was a big fan of vintage cars and was especially fond of the '47 Nash owned by Mr. George. Mr. Sloan probably wanted to take a look at the couple's antique car.

After giving last minute instructions to his wife, Mrs. Ethel and to Zach, Mr. Sloan escorted Mr. George and Mrs. Bessie to his car a 1965 Chevrolet Impala.

A feisty Mrs. Cross headed straight for the front seat. This was fine with Mr. Sloan but long held southern racial tradition might have her seated in the back.

Zach was in the back of the store patiently waiting on a group of small boys. The three of them were in the throes of a major decision on how to spend the sixty cents they had to share. With Zach being otherwise occupied this left Mrs. Ethel to wait on us.

I was a little uneasy around Mrs. Ethel. I don't know why I felt that way because she was very sweet and not at all stand-offish. The only thing I can think of is that she wasn't in the store that often and I wasn't quite use to her. I was basically a shy person and it sometimes took a while before I warmed up to new people.

"Why you young ladies look very pretty today."

"Thank you, Mrs. Sloan. Could we have two fudge bars, please?" I gave my sister the task of speaking to her.

"You sure can. Let me give you some napkins you don't want to get chocolate drippings on those nice dresses."

Well, that was a very gracious gesture on her part.

"Aw don't be so nice to that one, Mom. She's just gonna wipe her hands on her dress anyway!"

Zach was pointing to me as he made his way to the front. The three little fellas he'd been helping seemed quite pleased with their purchase as they sauntered out of the store.

"Oh, now, Zach she seems like a very nice young lady I'm sure she'd never do anything like that."

"He's just mad because I caught him wiping his nose on his sleeve one day!" I had to retaliate.

"Well now THAT I would believe. He can be a little pig around the house! Mrs. Ethel was on my side. Score one for me!

"OOh Zach, she GOT you!" With my last zing, Charlene and I got our chocolate bars and started to leave the store.

"Thank you girls!" "Y'all have a good day now!"

"You too, Mrs. Ethel. BYE PORKY PIG!"

Zach laughingly made snorting pig sounds as we left the store.

"I didn't know that you and Zach were such good friends." Charlene couldn't wait to start teasing me.

Before I had a chance to respond, Charlene's friend, Michelle called to us from across the street. She was right on time because I didn't feel like having this conversation with my sister.

"Hey Charlene, are y'all just getting out of church?"

"A little while ago, girl, what are you doing home so early?" Michelle and her family went to a little church out in Robinson Addition and they held services until two on most Sundays.

"Rev. Perkins let out services a little early because so many people were going to the wedding at First Baptist."

"Dang, Is EVERYBODY going to that wedding?!" Charlene was still being quite careful not to spill on her dress. The napkins acquired at Sloan's store were proving to be quite useful.

"I heard Carla Thomas was going to sing." Okay, I was lying, but they were ignoring me, so I had to say something.

Both Michelle and my sister stopped talking and looked at me like I had developed another set of eyes.

"Doris Marie now how you gonna stand there and tell a lie like that and ON A SUNDAY!"

Now, Michelle is fussing at me and she had to bring the Sabbath into it. I had forgotten that today was Sunday when I shot my mouth off telling that humongous lie.

Daddy always taught us to: REMEMBER THE SABBATH DAY AND KEEP IT HOLY. So my telling a known untruth even in' jest' was a fearsome thing that I quickly had to retract.

"Oh, y'all know I was just kidding." I quickly changed the subject by asking Michelle what she was wearing to the wedding.

"Mama bought me a real pretty outfit at a store in Memphis." Michelle's parents often went to Memphis to shop.

"Why did y'all go to Memphis? We got a Pennys here in town."

"They got more stuff at the stores in Memphis than here in town." My sister quickly chimed in to rescue me from looking so clueless. After all, everyone knew that a big city like Memphis would have more of a variety of everything.

"Come on we gotta go anyway." What is it about older sisters that makes them so bossy?

"Okay, see ya Michelle." We were about to turn and walk away when Charlene suddenly stopped to tell Michelle something she's forgotten.

"Guess who has a little crush on Doris Marie?" Charlene was grinning from ear to ear and I had no knowledge of what she was talking about.

"Who is it, Charlene?" The usually reserved Michelle was a little too giddy at the prospect of finding out something personal about me.

I was completely oblivious until I remembered where we had just come from and the brief playful exchange that had occurred.

Little did my sister realize that she had read the situation incorrectly. It wasn't Zach that had the crush on me, but the opposite. . . . I had the crush on him.

"Oh, Michelle, you should have seen the way Zach was being all sweet to Doris Marie." Lord Charlene was worst than Daddy in teasing me.

"He was teasing both of us. It wasn't just me. Michelle, you know how Zach can be sometimes."

"Yeah, sometimes he's very talkative and then sometimes he has next to nothing to say." Thankfully Michelle was trying to ease this searing pain of embarrassment I was going through. At least I thought she was.

"Charlene, stop teasing your little sister. You know that boy doesn't like her. Besides, Bobby Joe would beat the fire out of Zach for messing with his woman!"

With that last bit of humiliation the both of them nearly killed themselves laughing. I took that as my cue to leave.

"Wait up, Doris Marie! Don't go running off just because we were making fun of you. . . You know we didn't mean it." Charlene moved quickly to catch up with me.

The phrase "You know we didn't mean it," did not make me feel better. I don't think it has ever made anyone feel better, at least not the person whose feelings were just hurt. It just makes the person who uttered the crushing remark feel a little less guilty about saying it.

I did wait on my sister and readily let the remark go. Partly because I knew she and Michelle really were kidding and also because we still had a small distance to go before getting home. I didn't want to walk all that way silent in the hot sun which would only serve to make the journey much longer.

The 'IT' Girls

We had made it about halfway down Calhoun Street when we ran into Katie Donnelly, Deidre Hamilton, and Rebecca Watson better known as the 'IT' girls.

Every economic sector and every ethnic group has a crew like this bunch. They were a nasty, mean-spirited group of girls who quite frankly thought they were "IT".

"Hey, Charlene and Doris Marie. Where's your shadow, Lillian?" It was Rebecca Watson. To the untrained ear this greeting sounded innocent enough, but to those of us who knew her, there was a distinct hint of sarcasm.

"I'll probably see Lillian later this afternoon. First Baptist hasn't let out yet."

"Charlene, can't you speak?" This was Katie Donnelly. Neither Charlene nor I liked her. She always had some smart remark and liked to 'loud-talk' a person by pointing out some imperfection and announcing it to anyone within ear shot.

"Hello Katie, Deidre, and Rebecca. I DID speak before, you just didn't hear me." My sister's response also held a sarcastic tone.

"Y'all going to the wedding this afternoon?" I interjected just to quickly change the mood of the conversation.

"I guess if y'all go you're going to wear what you got on, uh?" There she goes again with the smart remark. Well, Katie is nothing if not consistent.

"Don't worry about what we're wearing. You just take care of your own self, Katie Donnelly!" My sister's patience was wearing very thin.

"Ain't nobody worried 'bout what you wearing, Charlene. I just asked a question!" Katie rolled her eyes while she delivered her heated answer to Charlene.

Just as my sister was about to open her mouth and really belt one out to Katie up walks Mrs. Ethel Mae Reeves.

"Well, hello girls. Don't you all look cute in your Sunday frocks. Well, Miss Charlene, I see that Gurt really fixed you and your sister up. Your hair looks great as always." This quickly brought us back to the reality of Sunday and diffused the tense situation.

"Hello, Mrs. Ethel. Hey, Mrs. Ethel" The group answered in their best innocent-type voices.

As usual Mrs. Ethel looked stunning from head to toe. She wore a beautiful peach colored short sleeved dress which was cinched and belted at the waist. The black patent purse and heels with leopard trimming matched the pill-box type hat she wore atop her recently hot curled hair. Mrs. Ethel's outfit was topped off with a black umbrella she used to shield her from the afternoon sun.

"As I was walking up, I heard you all talking about the wedding this afternoon. If you are going you probably need to get home to freshen up." Translation: I heard you arguing from down the street. Go home before you get into some serious trouble!

With that exchange completed, our individual groups dispersed to move onto our intended destinations. Personally, I was glad that Mrs. Ethel showed up to squelch the situation.

These girls had a reputation of picking on anyone who didn't quite fit their mold of normal. Some time ago, they had decided that my sister did not fit that mold. So whenever they had the chance, they would do what they could to chip away at her self esteem.

Because of this, my sister had very little patience where the 'IT' girls were concerned.

Wedding Preperatons

Charlene's anger at the "IT" girls was soon replaced with an all consuming joy after seeing Elliot's car parked in our front yard. It wasn't so much that she had a little crush on him, (which she did.) as she was looking forward to possibly attending the wedding with him and Velma.

It was a good thing that Elliot lived close by in Batesville. We would see him on an almost daily basis during this summer.

It seems that Elliot wasn't our only visitor, as Aunt Helen's car was also parked outside our house. Apparently, mama and I would be riding to the afternoon ceremonies with her. My father wasn't about to sit through something like a wedding unless it was a close family member.

When we got to the front porch we could hear the big radio blasting Rev. Williams' sermon courtesy of WDIA. Daddy frowned on our listening to secular music on a Sunday. So we mostly listened to 'DIA on Sundays because they only aired religious programming on the Sabbath.

Mama called us to her bedroom as soon as we came in. "What's this I'm hearing about the two of you practically fighting with some girls on Calhoun Street?"

"Did Mrs. Ethel call you? If she did, she is not telling the whole story. We weren't fighting anybody." Charlene answered first. This was probably because Mama seemed to be mostly looking at her while she was tearing into us.

"Mrs. Ethel? Now you know Mrs. Ethel Mae Reeves isn't about to get on the phone and spread some mess like this."

Mama defended Mrs. Ethel so vehemently it was almost as if she was insulted for her at my sister's accusation.

"Now, I want the two of you to think very carefully. Whose house were you standing in front of while arguing with those girls?"

"Mrs. Molly Sanders!" I blurted out the answer seconds before my sister could even form the words in her mouth.

Mrs. Molly Sanders, a tall, skinny, middle age woman with stringy shoulder length hair, was the neighborhood GOSSIP. Every community has one and Molly Sanders was ours.

She treated this position as if it was her job and she was very good at it. The only difference being is that on an actual job, she'd have days off and a vacation. Not Mrs. Molly. She was on her job as the neighborhood gossip twenty-four seven.

There was an ironic twist though to her snoopiness. It appears that Mrs. Molly Sanders had a handle on the lives of everyone else in the neighborhood except her husband, Mr. Irving Sanders (a well known skirt chaser and drunkard.)

"Mama we weren't fighting. You know who it was, Katie Donnelly and her 'snooty' bunch. They were picking with Charlene." I had to speak up and let Mama know we were justified in our verbal exchange with the 'IT' girls.

"What were they saying to you Charlene?" Now mama was getting really concerned about her daughter and irritated with the girls.

"The 'IT' girls were just trying to make fun of my dress and I exchanged words with that Katie Donnelly." Charlene proceeded to tell how she was about to light into the girls when Mrs. Ethel walked up to the group.

"She spoke up for herself, Mama. We weren't fighting but we did get kinda loud." I was glad to see that mama was looking more at ease.

"Mrs. Ethel was coming home from church. When she saw us arguing she stopped to talk to us and settled the whole thing."

"Well, Mrs. Molly called me and according to her y'all were about to really go at it!" I saw Aunt Helen give mama a look like 'I told you Molly Sanders was exaggerating the whole thing!'

"Who are the "IT" girls anyway?" Aunt Helen had sat by patiently, but that hint of red in her face gave way to a growing anger inside.

While Mama proceeded to fill in Aunt Helen on just who and what the "IT" girls were, Charlene and I went to the kitchen to get a little of mama's Sunday dinner. I was ready to put the whole thing behind me.

"I can't stand Katie and Rebecca 'nem. They think they're something!" I thought my sister had let the matter go, but apparently it was still bothering her.

"Forget them! You know Rebecca wouldn't be saying anything if she wasn't around Deidre and Katie." I wasn't just saying this either, because Rebecca could be a decent person when she wasn't around the others. I don't think that Rebecca felt that she measured up to the rest of the others. She always felt the need to prove herself worthy by going along with their hateful behavior.

Unfortunately, picking on the two of us was their pet project. It seems that the "IT" girls always had to get their little 'shots' in and their relentless taunts were especially harsh towards my sister.

We had just sat down to eat when daddy came to the kitchen demanding one of us to fix him a plate.

"Elliot, you want some food?" Daddy was being unusually polite in his invitation. Normally, that sentence would have begun with the word "Boy" and not 'Elliot'.

"No sir, I'm good. We will probably get something after the wedding this afternoon."

"Oh 'WE' will get food later on at the wedding. Well, I hope 'WE' don't get any foolish ideas while 'WE' are at the wedding!"

Daddy's joking but quite serious words to Elliot and Velma made Charlene and me forget about our earlier incident.

Velma who had been sitting at the dining room table with Elliot only looked up for a moment. She was too busy looking through the letters from Elliot's 'little brothers.'

Elliot belonged to the Omega Psi Phi Fraternity and he had his pledges write Velma letters telling her why she should marry him. Needless to say, Daddy had no idea what was in those envelopes.

"Girls, y'all better freshen up if you're riding with me and Aunt Helen." Mama yelled from her bedroom to remind us of the afternoon's events.

Charlene and I had to quickly (and carefully) finish piling on the greens and chicken.

"What about Larry Wayne? Where is he anyway?" In all the excitement of the day, I had completely forgotten about him.

Daddy answered saying that he let Larry Wayne spend the afternoon at his friend's Kurt Ross' house.

"Mama, could Lillian go with us to the wedding?" I hadn't really talked to Lillian about this, but I was sure she'd go.

"Well, call her right now and she has to be here in fifteen minutes ready to go!" Mama couldn't have been surprised by this request.

I proceeded to go straight to the phone and dialed her number.

"Hello, Mrs. Jarrett, could I speak to Lillian?"

"I was just about to call over to Emma's house to tell her to come home. She's got to freshen up for the wedding. Are y'all going to the wedding?"

"Yes ma'am, I was just calling to see if Lillian could ride with us."

"I'm afraid not dear. Lillian and I are going to ride with Mrs. Jo Ann and her family.

"Well thank you anyway Mrs. Jarrett. Would you tell Lillian that I called?" I was rather envious that Lillian gets another chance to spend time with Gary and Doll.

"I sure will sweetie. Say Hello to your mother for me and I will see you guys at the Wedding."

"Lillian wasn't at home?" I guess the disappointment on my face was easily read by Charlene.

I explained that Lillian was over to Emma's house and we would probably see her at the wedding.

Velma excused herself from Elliot to get ready for the afternoon's festivities. Elliot reluctantly decided to go to the kitchen and spend some time with his probable future father-in-law.

Daddy was sitting at the table having his favorite buttermilk and cornbread drink.

"Have a drink son it's good for you!" Daddy had his trademark mischievous smile on.

"No Sir, I think I'll pass. But I will have some coffee if some is available."

"Oh, you are just like my wife. She loves her coffee." Daddy took another big gulp of his ice cold concoction.

"Boy, why are you going to this wedding? You know these people?" Daddy already knew the answer to this question, he was making polite conversation.

"I don't know the bride but the groom and I are in the same fraternity.

"Then why on earth are you going?" He said still smiling mischievously. Daddy knew Elliot was most likely going only on Velma's request. He was just having some good nature fun at Elliot's expense.

"Your daughter wanted to go, so I said that I would take her." Elliot realized that Daddy was just having fun with him and that made the both of them laugh.

Charlene and I had long since left the room and proceeded to freshen up our hair and wash our face. Luckily, the fudge bars that we'd gotten earlier at Sloan's grocery didn't spill onto our dresses.

After mama helped us with our hair and brushed off our dresses to help give them a fresh look, Charlene and I were ready to go. It didn't take mama long to finish her hair and makeup, while Aunt Helen decided to reapply her lipstick and perfume all the while giving the rest of us fashion tips.

"Now Girls, put a little perfume on your wrists. . . . not too much. You don't want the person sitting beside you to be overwhelmed with the scent. Gurt, give these Girls some vaseline for their legs. Doris Marie's legs are looking kinda ashy." This was a treat for my Aunt Helen. With so many men in her house, she never had a chance to share her fashion and make-up tips.

It was kind of fun getting dressed with Mama. I felt grownup when Aunt Helen demonstrated how to use perfume properly. After a while, it felt more like one of us was preparing for our own wedding as opposed to attending one.

Moments later, with the final details completed, three of us head for Aunt Helen's car. Mama looked fabulous in the new outfit that Velma bought for her birthday.

Charlene got in the car with Elliot and Velma. She was so excited that she almost got in the front seat. Of course, my older sister was having none of that. Velma quickly steered her to the rear of the car.

A Wedding To Remember

By the time we arrived at First Baptist both sides of Second Street had almost filled with cars. Most were freshly polished local cars. There were a number of brand new cars with out of town license plates.

"Hey Gurt! Hey Helen!" Just as we were emerging from our cars, Mrs. Craft was also exiting hers.

Mrs. Craft had taught first grade at WF Branch School for as long as I could remember. She (along with Mrs. Betty Taylor of Newport High) stands out as my most memorable teachers during my career as a student. The former showered her students with love while cleverly sneaking in the three R's. The latter fed my interest in the history of this country which left me with an insatiable appetite for more.

On a lighter note, I do remember getting one spanking from Mrs. Craft which hurt my pride worlds more than my derriere!

"Hello, Mrs. Craft. I see you're going to the big shindig too."

Mama had great admiration for Mrs. Craft because she was a teacher. During the 1960s educators were still held in high regard and possessed a certain elevated status in our community.

"I have never seen so many cars in my life!" By now Mrs. Craft has joined us in walking to the Church.

"Well, hey there Doris Marie! Gurt, this girl has grown so 'til I barely recognized her."

"I'm going to eighth grade this year, Mrs. Craft." I quickly belted out that bit of information while Mrs. Craft responded with an approving smile and the standard teacher words of encouragement.

Mama, Aunt Helen, and Mrs. Craft continued on in conversation until they reached the steps of the church. At that time, they maintained a silence that would suggest that they were attending a funeral instead of a wedding.

A young man dressed in what we later learned was a dashiki, escorted us to a nearly empty pew toward the middle. As we were being seated we noticed Mr. George and Mrs. Bessie Cross were already seated and chatting quietly with each other.

It was no surprise to see the snappy dressed elderly couple at the ceremony. The two were known to attend every wedding, funeral, graduation, or any other major event that occurred in our community.

Scanning the church, I could see Lillian and Emma sitting a few rows ahead of us and to the right. Lillian's mother and Mrs. Weston were sitting between the two of them. I'm sure this was not by accident. Mrs. Jarrett wanted to make sure that there would be no giggling or talking during the nuptials.

To my surprise, I didn't spot Doll and her husband with Mrs. Weston. I wondered where they were since Mrs. Jarrett said that they were riding with them.

"Doris Marie, who's that little girl sitting with Mrs. Jarrett and Lillian?" Mrs. Craft's expression suggested that even though she'd asked the question she had some vague idea as to who the person was.

I whispered the identity of Emma to Mrs. Craft. I reminded her that Emma had been in the class with me.

"Oh, I remember that little stinker!" Mrs. Craft had to cover her mouth in an effort to contain the laughter.

Just the use of the word 'stinker' said that Mrs. Craft recalled Emma's classroom and school yard high jinks. Her lack of elaboration on the subject showed a level of respect for Emma Jean. If Mrs. Craft had any other memories about her former student she would keep them to herself.

I however was having a small problem with the new arrangement. Lillian was my friend and all of a sudden she and Emma were thick as thieves.

Just then, Lillian and Emma turned around and gave me a big wave hello. This made me feel better. Maybe I hadn't lost my best friend after all.

More and more people were arriving. Everyone had the same look of awe with mouths open and jaws dropped at the elaborately decorated sanctuary.

There were large blue and white bows with a small spray of colorful flowers in the center. These arrangements were placed at the end of each pew.

Down the aisle between the pews was a white runner type rug covered with lilacs until it reached the place in front of the pulpit. This area continued the theme with ascending white candles on stands in a semicircle fashion.

By this time Charlene, Velma and Elliot had made it to the church and luckily found a spot almost directly behind us. Velma was in complete wonderment. She could only hope to have a wedding ceremony half as majestic as this one.

The families of the bride and groom were coming in. The first two pews of either side (and in the middle) were reserved just for them. As they slowly proceeded in, mama spotted Mrs. Richmond and her family.

Mrs. Richmond also saw Mama and gave her hair a quick Hollywood fluff after waving to her.

To mama's dismay, Mrs. Richmond had on a rather large hat which covered about half of her head. Mama was concerned that all of her work on Mrs. Richmond's hair might be hidden from view. Fortunately, her long locks fell down around her shoulders. People could still see some of mama's handiwork.

The church had now filled to its capacity and people were starting to stand at the back.

"Glad we got here when we did. I couldn't take that standing up." Aunt Helen didn't like to participate in anything that would involve her standing for long periods of time.

As if on cue, everyone turned around to see the groomsmen and brides maids slowly make their way down the aisle in a beautiful arm in arm procession. I didn't realize at the time, but the mystery of the whereabouts of Doll and her new husband was about to be solved. They were a part of the wedding procession.

The groomsmen dressed in white tuxedoes with powder blue cummerbunds, took their places at the altar. Following their lead, the bridesmaids who came dressed in powder blue strapless gowns also took their places at the altar. Each had their hair in a neatly coiffed afro which was distinct in their size and shape.

One bridesmaid's hair was even large enough to rival the size of a regulation basketball. The rest of the girls had medium sized round shaped afros which framed their faces and highlighted their sparkling smiles.

The girls also wore small white gardenias cleverly pinned on the left side of their head. This gave an additional unifying look to the group. It also helped to soften the image of a style (the afro) which had yet to be embraced by some of the older guests. I thought it looked great and the young ladies displayed an air of African pride about themselves as they walked down the aisle.

The groom, dressed in a black tuxedo, held a masterful stance at the altar. The soothing classical music that had been playing as the guests came in has now given way to The Wedding March.

Immediately and on cue the bride and her father appeared at the double doors.

The father is dressed in a dark blue suit with a small maroon colored flower in his lapel.

The bride looked spectacular in her long white, lace gown. It had beautiful long sleeves which were also lace. A powder blue sash sewed at the waist of her gown helped to complete her radiant look.

But none of these things compared to the beautiful bridal train which trailed the young bride while she effortlessly whisked her way down the aisle.

As we were standing for father and daughter to make their way to the altar, I witness two events which would stick with me for the remainder of the summer.

First, out of the corner of my eye, I could see my mother, Aunt Helen, and Mrs. Craft all teary eyed with hankies at the ready to dap their eyes. It was a beautiful ceremony and all, but I didn't see the need for the waterworks.

The other event involved Bobby Joe Walker. I swear to GOD this boy lives to torture me at every chance he gets!

Just as the father walks his daughter down the aisle to her future husband, I see Bobby Joe. And what's worse. . . . .he sees me!

He had me in a kind of stare at which I couldn't look away. Having me in his power, he mouths the words: I LOVE YOU DORIS MARIE! He then repeatedly points to the altar and then to me suggesting that we would be next.

And if that wasn't bad enough, he puts his big Bobby Joe lips together and blew me a kiss! I HATE HIM!

"Doris Marie, you seem to have an admirer." Aunt Helen would have to have seen that. Of course she would think it's cute, she doesn't have any daughters. Any kind of puppy love would seem cute to her.

"Helen, that's Bobby Joe Walker. And he's not Doris Marie's boyfriend. . . . but he sure wants to be."

Leave it to Mama to always come to my defense. Although in this case, she did manage to both defend me while also having a little fun at my expense.

"I remember when he had a little crush on her when they were in my class." Et tu, Mrs. Craft?

Man, that's been years ago! Teachers don't forget anything!

By now everyone had taken their assigned places at the altar. Just before taking his seat, the bride's father kisses her lightly on the forehead through her veil.

Some observers seemed to have a look of slight embarrassment. Maybe they thought that the father had committed a slight faux pas by not lifting the bride's veil.

I prefer to think that the lifting of the veil was an act that her father decided to leave to the new man in his daughter's life.

Admittedly, I'd never been to a wedding, but I had a vague understanding as to what to expect. Of course this knowledge was totally based on the weddings I'd seen on television which was always some exaggerated comical version of the truth.

For instance this wedding was nothing like the 'near miss' nuptials of Rob and Laura Petrie on the Dick Van Dyke Show. And it certainly wasn't the hillbilly version of Romeo and Juliet shown recently on the Andy Giffith Show.

Reverend Doctor Mitchell Brown administered the vows for the couple. The Reverend was the moderator for the District Baptist Congress and an old college classmate of Mrs. Richmond and her husband at AM&N.

"Do you Michael Lewis Powell, take thee Alice Rose Richmond to have and to hold from this day forward?" I don't know if it was the temperature inside the church or nervousness, but it took the groom a few seconds to answer.

It didn't take the bride anytime to respond. The minister barely had the words out of his mouth before the anxious bride had her "I DO" ready for him.

I had never seen anyone so beautiful. Alice's radiance literally burned right thru her veil.

Apparently, my mother and about every other mother in the room felt the same way, because there were tissues and hankies everywhere. . . . ...more waterworks.

Just after Minister Brown pronounces the couple as 'man and wife', the Best Man placed a small decorative broom on the altar in back of the new couple.

"And now Mr. and Mrs. Michael Powell will 'jump the broom' to holy matrimony!"

Now that was the strangest thing I had ever seen. Of all the weddings I had witnessed on television, I'd never seen anyone 'jump a broom' to become officially wed.

It was quite clear that I wasn't the only one shocked by the unconventional ending to the ceremony. The number of jaws dropped and perplexed looks on the faces of other observers says that they were also stunned by this unusual ritual.

I must say not everyone was stunned by this ritual. A number of older people had a kind of smile and a little chuckle after witnessing the event. I heard Mrs. Adele comment that her grandmother had told her about 'jumping the broom.'

But this was not to be the end to the surprise wedding practices we would witness. Once we went outside and the bride had thrown the bouquet, a number of young men dressed in purple and gold assembled onto the parking lot adjacent to the church.

In a straight line, they began to chant in unison the praises of their fraternity and of the bride and groom. In addition to the chanting, the young men also did a kind of stepping and hand gestures. . . . again all in unison. This was really a fantastic sight to see!

The bride and groom stood along the sideline with the rest of us to watch the exhibition. Suddenly, newly married Michael joined them in the stepping display and soon after we noticed Elliot had also joined the group. They were really very good. I learned later that these young men were all members of Omega Psi Phi, Elliot's fraternity.

Because of the huge number of wedding guests the only place in town where the reception could be held was the auditorium at Branch High School. Mama and Aunt Helen went to the gathering along with Mrs. Craft.

I was more than happy when Mama dropped me off at home. The wedding was magnificent. But I couldn't stand having these clothes on any longer even if Branch was just down the street from our house.

When I got inside I was surprised to see my sister sitting in the living room watching television. Apparently, Elliot and Velma had dropped her off while they went on to the reception.

"You didn't go to the reception with Elliot and Velma?" Charlene gave me a very harsh look.

"Well, if I'm sitting here I guess I didn't go. And neither did you while you trying to be funny."

"I really didn't want to go. I'm tired of these clothes. I got to get comfortable." I wasn't lying about that.

Charlene already had a piece of apple cobbler and a cold glass of milk on the coffee table in front of her. Something tells me that she wasn't missing the reception or Elliot and Velma not the least little bit. For a few brief moments, she had a great dessert the TV, and the whole house to herself. That is until I came home!

After changing into my everyday clothes, I went to the kitchen to get some of that cobbler and a glass of milk. The next step would be to join my sister in the living room with my snack.

If looks could kill, I would have died on the spot. Mimicking something a sibling (or friend) has done was a major snafu in kid etiquette.

If you dared to copy someone else's idea you were bound to hear the following sentence:

"You just did that 'cause you saw me doing it!"

A Visit To the Country

A rustling at the back door momentarily startled us until we realized that it was our father and Larry Wayne.

"Y'all put that food away and get ready to go." Daddy's stern voice told us to move quickly.

119

"This is your mother's last day of vacation, so let's give her a few more hours of freedom."

He didn't say where we were going, but it was a Sunday afternoon and our destination was a given.

We were headed for Augusta.

My father was raised in Augusta, Arkansas, A small town just 33 miles away.

Daddy's father, grandfather, and a host of other relatives still reside in and around the Augusta area.

For as long as I could remember, Daddy would pile us all into the car and head for Augusta, the 'Motherland'. This trip home would occur at least once a month.

Back in the day people didn't really worry about calling ahead to visit. . . . they would just show up.

It was getting later in the day, so the visit with our relatives would probably be limited to Papa Lonze and Papa Sol. These were my father's respective father and grandfather. I didn't mind visiting with my relatives, as a matter of fact, I rather enjoyed it.

However, I didn't care for the ride down there on a hot summer day. The 'Batmobile' (our car) had no air conditioning, so we had to ride with the windows down which could sometimes make for an uncomfortable journey.

"Y'all make sure you use the bathroom too." Daddy's mumbled words only served to remind us that neither Papa Sol nor Papa Lonzee had an indoor bathroom. As a result, we would have to use the dreaded outhouse.

As we head out of the car port Daddy makes a left toward Garfield. This was not the most direct way to Remmel which led to Highway 17.

"Daddy, you're going the wrong way." Larry Wayne blurted out what my sister and I had been thinking. The innocence of his young years enabled him to get away with the occasional inappropriately timed sentence.

"We're going to make a stop on Mason Street to see if your buddy Lillian wants to go with us." I was surprised because I hadn't called her about the trip.

It wasn't unusual for Lillian to accompany us on our Sunday trip. Quite often if she was visiting and Daddy suddenly decided to take us to Augusta, getting the okay was a simple phone call away.

"Hadn't seen much of your friend lately, I thought you might like for her to come along." This was really very thoughtful on the part of my father.

I didn't get a chance to speak with Lillian at the wedding. As far as I knew she might be with her mother at the reception.

Upon arrival to the Jarretts, we found Lillian and Emma Jean in the yard on the side of the house. They were sitting at the family picnic table gulping down two large bowls of Chocolate ice cream.

Having immediately spotted us, Lillian led the way to our car.

"Hey, Mr. Willie. Hey,Charlene and Doris Marie" At that point Lillian pushes her head inside toward Larry Wayne and gives him a big kiss.

"Hey Cutie!" Lillian loved to tease Larry Wayne. Sneaking up on him to give him a big kiss was her favorite form of loveable torture.

"Lillian, we were on our way to Augusta and wondered if you wanted to go." Seeing Lillian's company Daddy knew the answer to the question, but asked anyway out of politeness.

"Thanks Mr. Willie but I can't go because I have company." Lillian turns slightly to reveal Emma Jean standing in back of her. Emma Jean then gives a sheepish wave to us.

"Besides, Mama wanted me to stay here until she got back from the wedding reception. Say 'Hello' to Uncle Buddy for me!"

We said our 'good byes' to both Lillian and Emma Jean and proceeded onto the country.

"Doris Marie who is that little girl?" Daddy had seen Emma Jean around he just didn't know her name.

"That's Emma Jean Hines. She lives over in Calhoun Circle. Her father is Mr. Leroy Hines."

It's important to make the 'kin people' link when you're trying to get one person to remember another.

Thank God that Augusta is a short distance from Newport. It took us all of about 25 minutes to get there.

We were visiting Papa Lonzee and Mother Abbey who lived just outside of Augusta at the end of a long dirt road.

Going to visit the elderly couple down that long, dirt road could sometimes make an already hot day feel even hotter.

But travelling down country roads did have its positive side, they were ideal places for impromptu driving lessons.

121

Here is where Velma and Mama got their driving lessons. Velma did okay but mama. . . . well let's just say that we all appreciated life a little more after that adventure.

Once you got to Papa Lonzee's house it was like a step back in time. It wasn't so much the chickens and roosters that roamed their yard or the three goats that were fenced in behind their house.

It was the atmosphere of the home itself. It was filled with furnishings and pictures from a bygone era.

My favorite was their gramophone. It looked just like the one Donna Reed was playing in the movie 'It's a Wonderful Life.'

Another appealing feature was the multitude of pictures which lined the walls of both the living and dining rooms. There were even pictures on the walls in the kitchen and on the surfaces of different tables throughout the house.

A number of the beautifully framed black and white or sepia toned images on the walls were of adolescents and young adults. I was always amazed by the fact that a number of these vibrant, youthful images were of people I knew now as my aunts and uncles.

The most striking pictures were the individual portraits of Mrs. Abbey's parents. They were strategically placed above the others on the wall behind the sofa. The pictures looked as though they had been taken around the turn of the century probably between late 1890s and early 1900s.

"Hey y'all come on in here! Well, look here at Larry Wayne. . . . Boy you're growing like a weed!" The elderly couple's greetings suggested that they were genuinely glad to see us.

We responded appropriately as we greeted them with warm hugs and kisses.

"Willie, Where's Gurt?" Daddy proceeded to inform the two of the reasons for Mama's absence.

With that Charlene and I followed Daddy into the house. We left Larry Wayne outside who had already found a number of ways to amuse himself.

"Butterbean, Get these girls some cake." For a small frame woman, Mother Abbey had a voice that carried.

"No ma'am, those girls just had some cobbler at home. They don't need anything else." I hope she doesn't listen to Daddy and gives us some to take home.

"Okay, I tell you what, I'll wrap some up for you to take home."

"Thank you, Mother Abbey."

"Abbey, give Butterbean some of that bacon and ham from the freezer." Papa Lonzee was determined to load us up with food before we left there.

"We slaughtered a hog last week and we ain't gonna eat all that meat, so y'all might as well take some of it back with you."

This is what is known as 'Southern Hospitality' in its most sincere form. People in the country would take it as an insult if you didn't at least take something to eat before you left their home.

Daddy and Papa Lonzee decide to continue their conversation outside on the front porch. Charlene and I wandered into the kitchen with Mama Abbey while she cut and wrapped the meat for us.

"You girls help yourself to some lemonade." What a welcome relief. Even though they had two fans, only one was turned on at this time and we were starting to sweat.

I suspect that the heat was the reason why Daddy suggested that he and Papa Lonzee went outside. He also wanted to keep an eye on Larry Wayne.

Mama always said that once Larry Wayne got outside in the country that he just went 'buck wild.'

It was just too much space and too many distractions for a little boy. He will easily wear himself down and be too sleepy to take a bath tonight. As a result we would probably have a very cranky kid on our hands this evening.

While sitting at the kitchen table and enjoying our lemonade, I spotted a large box on the floor by the backdoor. It was halfway opened and I could see what appeared to be old black and white photos.

"Mother Abbey, could I see those pictures in that box?" I love old pictures.

Mother Abbey said it was okay for us to look over the pictures and to keep a close eye out for someone very special.

Charlene helped to lift the box onto the table. It was heavier than expected because the contents were more than just pictures. As it turns out there were at least six pairs of baby shoes, old vinyl records and a small music box.

We remembered to treat the treasures with the upmost respect and didn't just tear through the contents.

We saw a picture of two very proper young ladies with matching outfits and white gloves and purses. There was a picture of a baby in a rattan carriage and one of toddlers reluctantly holding each other's hands.

Mrs. Abbey perused the pictures with us. She had an interesting story to accompany each photo.

We soon came across the picture Mother Abbey must have been hinting at earlier. There it was in black and white and clear as day. . . my father as a teen ager in a 'zoot suit'.

Not too long ago Mama and I had watched a movie called 'Stormy Weather'. It was a 1940s movie and one of my mother's favorites. It starred one of my father's idols. . . . Cab Calloway. In the movie he wore a very 'sharp' 'zoot' suit. Mama said that daddy wore a suit like that when they dated. I didn't believe her because that didn't fit my father's personality. . . . or so I thought. But here he was in black and white. And to top it off, he was leaning and trying his hardest to look 'cool'!

Cool?! I love my father dearly, but cool is not a word that I could ever use to describe him.

With evidence in hand, Charlene and I rushed out to the front porch. Daddy and Papa Lonzee are still talking and watching Larry Wayne wear himself out playing in the yard.

"Daddy, guess what we got?" I had the picture hidden underneath my shirt.

"Well, I'm guessing it's not a snake." Now he knew better than that.

Mother Abbey trailed us onto the porch with lemonade for the men. "Butterbean, they got something of yours that you haven't seen in a very long time."

"Girl, What you got there?" Now his curiosity was really peaked.

"Ta-Dah!" Before I had a chance to tease him any further, Charlene snatched the picture from me and showed it to him.

"Daddy, I bet you thought you were a cool papa in that suit didn't you?!" I had to tease him.

"Girl, what you talkin' about! I was Sweet Papa Cool in my zoot suit. That's what I was wearing when I met your Mama!"

I couldn't help but wonder where my father would have worn this suit. And if he was wearing a zoot suit, how was my mother dressed?

"*Let me see! Let me see!*" *Larry Wayne ran onto the porch pushing his way between Mother Abbey and me to look at the picture.*

Of course as soon as he viewed the photo, Larry Wayne begins laughing and pointing at daddy.

"*Look at that hat!*" *It's a good thing that the picture was in black and white. I don't think that Larry Wayne could have taken it in color.*

"*Okay, Okay. Y'all have laughed enough. Say 'goodbye' to Papa Lonzee and Mother Abbey we have got to go.*"

"*Abbey, Make sure you get them that meat to take home.*"

Papa Lonzee wanted to make sure we got our package.

"*Here it is*" *Mother Abbey had already gotten the package while we were discussing the picture.*

Daddy carefully placed the meat in the trunk of the car. We then said our goodbyes and headed for Highway 17.

Daddy had spent a longer time at Papa Lonzee then he had anticipated. He decided to skip the visit with Papa Sol and Uncle Buddy and head directly for Newport.

There was still a glow of daylight when we set out for home. That seems to be the best time of day for me. It's not quite night and the day is just minutes away from being just a memory.

The late evening air blowing throughout the car felt soothing as it whisked across my face. As usual whenever we come back from any trip Larry Wayne has gone fast to sleep. He had been running around for most of the day and now that he's still he goes out like a light.

The Proposal

Why is it, that it always seems that it takes less time returning from a trip than it does to go somewhere? We had only been driving for what felt like a few minutes when there we were pulling into our carport.

As we pulled in, we could see the kitchen light on. Walking onto the back porch, we heard familiar voices and the sound of mama laughing uncontrollably. Upon entering the kitchen we find Velma and Elliot sitting with Mama drinking coffee and eating peach cobbler.

"*Where'd that cobbler come from?*" *Larry Wayne's eyes lit up and all sleep was removed after seeing the sweet treats.*

"*I made two cobblers and had one hidden away.*" *Mama knew all too well the voracious appetites of her family.*

Daddy proceeded to put the food away that we'd gotten from Mother Abbey while Mama heated up the coffee and the cobbler. Velma and Elliot excused themselves and went to the living room to 'watch' Ed Sullivan.

While Mama, Daddy and Larry Wayne were in the kitchen, Charlene decided to beat the rush for the bathroom and go ahead and get her bath.

I decided to take my cobbler to my bedroom and eat it while reading my comic books. It had cooled off a little and the fan brought in a welcome breeze which stirred throughout the room.

I loved my sister dearly, but I also loved the times when I could have our room all to myself. There was a unique kind of quietness that existed when the room held only one occupant. Besides on a warm summer night, I was glad to have the fan all to myself if only for a few minutes.

Suddenly Larry Wayne raced back to my room. He headed straight for my bed and started to bounce up and down. He had that look on his face that said that he was privy to information that I didn't know, but would love to find out.

"*Guess what Elliot just asked Daddy?*" *Larry Wayne could hardly contain his enthusiasm.*

"*Boy, this better be good 'cause I know you know better than to jump up and down on my bed!*"

Larry Wayne proceeds to tell me the most unexpected news. Elliot had asked Daddy if he could marry Velma!

Larry Wayne continued to say that Mama was happy about the idea but Daddy was not. It was at this point that Mama made Larry Wayne leave the room while the four of them discussed Elliot's proposal.

I decided to tip toe to the small hallway that separated the kitchen from the bathroom and Velma's bedroom. This was also the place where a large dresser drawer was kept. I could easily squat down beside it and still hear the conversation between the adults in the kitchen area.

"*Elliot, you know I like you a lot son, but my daughter is going to college. Marriage at such an early age might interfere with that.*"

Although I couldn't see my father's face, I could hear the seriousness in his voice.

"Willie, they're not getting married right away. This is only an engagement which could last for some time.... right, Velma?" Mama was trying very hard to reassure my father their daughter's education would not be interrupted. She also wanted the young couple to see that she was okay with their future nuptials.

"I still don't like it. Velma you are too young to even be thinking of marriage." It was clear that my father was none too ready to let go of his oldest child. He was just getting used to the fact that she was going off to school in a couple of months.

"Velma, why don't the two of you go over to Laura's for a while? I need to talk to your daddy for a minute." With that my sister and possible future brother-in-law reluctantly left the room.

Just then Mama peers over the dresser drawers and informs me that I had five seconds to get back to my room.

I move away far enough so as to be out of sight range, but still within earshot. Mama poured more coffee for her and Daddy and proceeded to remind him of what an energetic and goal oriented person Elliot was.

She also reminded him of how much Elliot and Velma adored each other. Daddy had to admit that he had admired Elliot. Mama reminded Daddy that Elliot had been nothing but a respectable young man since he and Velma met.

Charlene finally emerged from the bathroom and Mama had me to run bath water for Larry Wayne. She had paused her conversation with Daddy long enough to make sure I carried out her orders. It was getting late and past experience with Larry Wayne says that if we don't get him in that tub soon, he will get too cranky to go at all.

I quickly got Larry Wayne ready for his bath. Just as we had feared he was in his cranky mode. He had fallen to a light sleep when I left the room to listen in on the grown-ups discussion. I had to wake him up and make sure he had his night clothes to put on after his bath.

As I headed for my room after getting Larry Wayne situated, I could still hear Mama and Daddy discussing Elliot and Velma. By the sound of it, Daddy was coming around and was open to the idea of the two being engaged.

"I guess it will be alright. Elliot has a good head on his shoulders and wants to do something with his life." Daddy sounded like he had talked himself into the new arrangement.

"Willie, like I said, this is just an engagement, marriage is down the road a piece."

Mama and Daddy's voices soon became a bit softer as it often did when they decided that their conversation was for their ears only.

I finally got a chance to fill Charlene in on the exciting news about Velma and Elliot. Needless to say, she was on cloud nine with the prospect of having Elliot as a member of our family.

Later on while taking my bath, I thought about the different roads on which my sister was about to travel. I didn't realize it then, but this was just the first of many dramatic changes my family would encounter throughout the coming years.

We welcomed and praised God for those changes that brought joy to our family. We prayed for strength to endure the heart breaks and losses that is the inescapable fate of us all.

CHAPTER 8

Preparing For The Fourth Monday, July 3

"Make sure you take that chicken down at around nine o'clock. It should be thawed out by the time I get home this afternoon."

In the excitement of last night I forgot one very important fact: Mama's vacation was over and she was headed back to work this morning.

She was yelling out the usual rules for the days when neither she nor Daddy was at home.

They were pretty standard rules which were maintained in most homes of that time:

There was no company until the she came home

(Your best friend might visit briefly, but only in the afternoon)

No leaving the house until mama came home

No cooking on the stove (didn't apply to older teenagers)

No playing on the phone

DON'T OPEN THE DOOR TO STRANGERS!

In addition to enforcing and following the house rules, Mama had a major assignment for Velma today. She had to take us kids uptown for our Fourth-of-July outfits.

I always looked forward to this outing. I didn't mind shopping with mama, but when I shopped with Velma I felt more grown-up. She pretty much let me pick out my own clothes.

Mama was out of the house by ten to seven and had to clock in at the top of the hour. Luckily GPW Nursing Home was just around the corner from where we lived. She always made it in record time. It's probably because she did a walk-quick walk combo to get there. After years of practice, Mama now had the 'house to work' timing down to perfection.

Velma got up a few minutes after Mama left for work. Even though she had a full day ahead of her, she seemed to be in a great mood.

I'm certain she was still riding high from the wonderful memories of last night. She's probably thinking of the elaborate changes her life was about to take and welcoming it with wide open arms. While I drifted off to sleep last night, I remember thinking how different Velma's life would be just one year from now.

At the most she would be a married college sophomore and at the least she'd be an engaged college sophomore. Either way within a year's time there would be a significant change in her life.

"Y'all better get up and get to moving." Velma's tone wasn't quite as stern as it normally was when she bellowed out our morning instructions.

"Velma and Elliot sitting in a tree K-I-S-S-I-N-G," I could hear Larry Wayne teasing his big sister all the way back in my room.

"Larry Wayne, you need to be quiet with your little mannish self." Larry Wayne had wandered into the kitchen and greeted Velma with his 'kissing' poem.

"I'm just playing with you, Girl." Larry Wayne knew his status in the family as the youngest would assure him a quick forgiveness. Besides, it is never a good idea to anger your older siblings when the parents aren't there to defend you. We could make his life quite unpleasant.

Charlene soon made her way to the kitchen after washing up for breakfast. Before leaving our bedroom she reminded me of our Fourth of July shopping trip with Velma today. She knew this would light a fire under me and we could start our day much quicker.

It wasn't long after Charlene abandoned the bathroom that I went in to wash for breakfast. By the time I entered the kitchen, breakfast was on the table and everyone was deep into a lively conversation.

"Will you and Elliot live here when you get married?" Larry Wayne was deadly serious. It was as though he was trying to get a mental picture of the coming events.

Velma took a moment to answer.

"Larry Wayne, Elliot and I aren't getting married right away. It might be next year or it might be two years from now."

"When we do marry, we won't be staying here because we'll have our own place."

"But we will be coming here for visits and you can come to visit us. That'll be fun, right?!"

Larry Wayne's face seemed to emit an honest sigh of relief. I think he really was concerned about his sister being stolen away by Elliot.

"Okay. Okay, new topic. I called Laura and she will be here at about ten o'clock to take us to town. Since I have to go to work at two—thirty, we need to finish cleaning the house as soon as possible. This way we'll have time for shopping and I'll be home in plenty of time for work."

I was finally off kitchen duty and passed the baton on to Charlene. Today my job was to clean up the living room and my bedroom. Velma cleaned her room, bathroom, and she had to dust mop the house. Larry Wayne had to make up his bed. A job he purposely messed up every day so that one of us would come behind him and complete the task correctly.

Velma turned on the big radio in the living room. It was already tuned in to WDIA. It was our policy (as it is with most teenagers) to blast our music while we cleaned the house. Of course, we could only do this if mama and daddy wasn't at home.

Listening to Chris the Burner Turner lay on stacks and stacks of hit after hit helped to take the sting out of the drudgery of housework. Larry Wayne was trying to sing along with Stevie Wonder's 'I Was Made To Love Her.' He keeps messing up because he can never quite remember the words, so he makes up his own version of the song!

We were dressed and ready to go when Laura arrived at a few minutes past ten. She was quick to inform us that we had all the time in the world, because she was in no hurry. Laura worked in the laundry at the McAllister Motor Inn on Highway 67. She could be very generous with her time because she didn't have to go to work until three thirty.

We would start off by going to Fred's Dollar Store first. We could size up the merchandise and look to see if we could find a fitting set for the Fourth. The best thing about Fred's was that the clothes were VERY reasonably priced.

We arrived at Fred's which was located on Second Street a few doors down from Newport Hospital. Because it's a holiday, the store was pretty full of shoppers.

While Velma and Laura cart Larry Wayne off to the boys section, Charlene and I walked over to the racks for young girls and junior miss.

I was hoping to find a shorts set and matching pair of thongs (flip-flops.) My favorite colors were yellow and blue so I didn't think I'd have any problem in finding an outfit. Charlene's taste ran similar to mine, but she also had a penchant for red and khaki. She was alone on that one as I hated the color red with a passion and I always thought khaki was dull.

Velma told us to take our time and look around.

"Don't make any snap decisions because we're also going to Penny's."

I knew that we'd go to Penny's, but we would most likely wind up back here. The clothes were nicer at Penny's, but they were also higher priced. To be honest I didn't mind getting an outfit from Fred's. Spending less money on clothes meant more money on a pair of thongs or sneakers and possibly a comic book or Mad Magazine at Ryan's Drug Store.

We searched through the racks of clothes as though we were searching for the treasures of King Tut. Yet our frantic search yielded few hopefuls.

I was about to give up when I found the most perfect ensemble. A yellow shorts set with tiny colorful flowers lining the borders of the top and bottom. It was just my size (girls' twelve). Velma, playing her usual mother role, made me try it on to be certain of the fit.

The set cost seven dollars and ninety-five cents. As luck would have it, I also found a pair of yellow flip-flops for two dollars.

Laura even found a matching yellow headband and bought it for me. She said I needed it to complete my outfit.

It didn't take long to find clothes for Larry Wayne. Generally speaking, little boys could care less about new clothes and he was no exception to that rule. A pair of khaki shorts and a blue and white striped 'Opie Taylor' type shirt and Larry Wayne was good to go.

Charlene was adamant about going to JC Penny's, because she couldn't find anything to suit her in Fred's. So, with packages in hand, we loaded up the car and headed for Front Street.

Front Street was alive with a steady stream of people darting in and out of the stores. Although we didn't find a parking place directly in front of Penny's, we weren't too far away. When we finish shopping it will still be just a short stroll down to the restaurant.

Since Larry Wayne and I had made our purchases, Velma gave the okay to our walking down to Ben Franklin's Five and Ten cents store. I was looking for a paddle ball while Larry Wayne just wanted to find candy preferably Red Hots.

This Ben Franklin store was a particularly large one, even for a small town like Newport. It had the usual eye catching items as you entered the store like framed pictures, knickknacks, and home décor. Shelves parked in front of the cash register contained Life and Look magazines.

There were also shelves which held small amounts of the penny candy children sought while shopping with their mothers.

"Larry Wayne, come with me while I look for a paddle ball." I always liked to keep him close by otherwise he will wander away without me.

"Could I get one too?"

Just then a thought hit me. If Larry Wayne was asking for something that I still had an interest in owning, I've clearly gotten too old for this activity.

"I tell you what, Larry Wayne. I'll buy this one for you and I'll get something else.

I knew just what that something else was too. . . an autograph book. Some of the older girls had them and they seemed like a lot of fun.

The point of the book was to collect fun little notes like:
"2sweet, 2 be, 4gotten."

Most girls used their books to get as many autographs as possible. I think I'm going to go a different route and go for 'quality' and not 'quantity'. I might get a few older kids to sign my book or maybe even a teacher.

Larry Wayne found his Red Hots and I located the autograph book and paddle ball. He wanted to play with it immediately. I told him to wait until we got home. Mama would never allow us play with toys in the store. She said the clerks would look at you as though you weren't going to pay for the item. She hated that.

Just as we were approaching the counter with our purchases, Velma came in to hurry us along.

"Y'all ready? We've finished shopping and ready to go and eat. Larry Wayne, You know Mama does not want you eating all that candy!"

"You're always bossing people around! Could we go ahead and buy it anyway and you can keep it until tomorrow okay?" Larry Wayne could not lose his Red Hots and was willing to cut any kind of a deal to keep them.

"Okay, Okay! You can buy the candy. But you cannot have it until tomorrow." Velma was unyielding on that point.

With that, Larry Wayne turns and gives me a slight wink. He knows all he has to do is give Mama some big sob story and she will override Velma's orders and let him have his cherished treats.

It was getting close to lunch and Ted's Lunchroom was quickly filling up with customers.

We were really hoping to find a spot. A table was being cleared just as we strode thru the door and Larry Wayne made an immediate sprint for it.

"Larry Wayne, get back over here!" Both of my sisters spoke in loud whispers and motioned for our little brother to retreat.

Larry turned around and readied himself for an argument when he suddenly realized why his steps were halted. The area that had been cleared was in the "white section" of the restaurant.

"Boy, c'mon here, you know better than that." Velma quickly redirected our misguided little brother to the appropriately hued part of Ted's Lunch Room.

"We should go ahead and sit down just to see what would happen." Well, it seems that the tiniest member of our group is becoming quite the pint sized militant.

"Larry Wayne, sit your little narrow behind down before you get us all in trouble." Oddly enough this bit of direction came from Laura.

"Yeah, stop trying to stir up trouble, you little militant." Velma wasn't really angry with Larry Wayne. . . none of us were.

As a matter of fact we found it sort of amusing.

What would they have done if Larry Wayne actually sat in the 'wrong' section?

I doubt anything would have happened. It's 1967 and The Civil Rights Bill has long been signed into law. So, we actually had the right to sit anywhere we chose.

It would have been the talk of the town if we purposely sat in the wrong section and challenged the system.

On the other hand, it could have turned out to be 'much ado about nothing.' I don't think the patrons or the owners of Ted's would have said or did anything if we sat in the 'wrong place.'

CHAPTER 9

It's The Fourth Of July!! Tuesday, July 4

Mama left for work at the usual time but, not before doling out her usual litany of house instructions. Because today was a holiday she had added one or two more:

"Y'all know not to leave this house before I get home this afternoon."

"Make sure you hurry and get up. It's a holiday and company may be coming from out of town."

Out of town guests for us usually meant our Memphis or Augusta relatives. I highly doubt that we will see them today.

Of course, there was that odd chance of seeing some long lost relative from St. Louis or Chicago. Another scenario has a former childhood friend of my parents dropping in for an unexpected visit.

Laura came by promptly at one forty-five to take Velma to work.

While hurrying out the door, Velma made sure we revisited Mama's house rules. She reminded us that since she had to leave, we were under no circumstances to have any company what so ever.

This wasn't anything we could get away with anyway. Mama was notorious for making repeated calls to the house whenever we were home without official adult supervision. Also, there were many eyes all up and down Clay Street who both monitored and reported any strange happenings going on throughout the neighborhood.

Toward the afternoon we took advantage of being unsupervised by raiding the refrigerator for cold chicken, potato salad and bar-be-que baked beans. There was also chocolate and strawberry ice cream in the freezer for dessert.

We gathered in the living room to watch reruns of I LOVE LUCY. They were showing the 'Vitameatavegamin' episode which was a favorite of mine second only to the Cuban Pete episode.

The phone rings and as we suspected it was Mama calling to check up on us.

"I'll be home in a little bit. Y'all make sure to keep the back door and front screen door locked and NO COMPANY!"

Charlene had answered the phone as it is the custom that the eldest usually mans the phone when adults aren't present.

"Mama, can I go out to Jacksonport with Michelle and her family when you get home?" Charlene was using the oldest kid trick in the book. Ask a parent a question when they are really busy hoping they will say yes just to get rid of you.

"No, You will ride with Velma and Elliot along with your sister and Larry Wayne." Mama did not fall for the old 'distract the parent' routine.

By this time, Larry Wayne had made a pallet on the floor and was fast asleep with a belly full of junk food. Not only was he stuffed with mama's food, but Velma had released his candy she'd held captive from yesterday.

Just minutes before Mama was scheduled to arrive home, Charlene and I quickly cleaned any debris we had left while pigging out. This was also the time to put on the clothes we'd purchased on yesterday.

It was our intention to be 'sitting on ready' when mama came through the front door. The Fourth of July Holiday was coming to a rapid end. We needed to get out on our bikes to cruise the neighborhood for fun and certain adventure.

Mama was a bit later than expected. She had stopped by Aunt Helen's for a few minutes. The family had grilled quite a feast and Auntie urged her to not only taste but bring some samples home for Daddy. Aunt Juanita was also there visiting with Aunt Helen.

Because of work and family obligations neither mama nor Auntie got a chance to see their baby sister that often. Today, Aunt Juanita was there with her two 'play kids' Rachel and Desmond Nelson. They were the children of friends of Aunt Juanita who lived in St. Louis. Because she never had any children, Aunt Juanita sort of adopted the youngsters as her own.

After a while I heard voices outside in the front yard. I rushed to the porch and saw mama talking with Gail who was holding newborn baby Antoinette.

"Is the baby sleeping pretty well through the night?" Mama reached for the baby and immediately started to tug playfully at her tiny little hands and feet.

"She's sleeping very well most of the time. That is when Glen will let her sleep. Mrs. Gurt, Glen wants to play with the baby all the time! He'll wake her up just to play with her!"

"Give him some time he's just being a new father." Mama wanted to reassure the new mother that this behavior is pretty normal.

"Gail, come on in and get some ice cream and cool off. The kids are getting ready to visit with their friends. I could use some company before Willie gets home."

Right about that time I walked down the front porch steps to greet mama and Mrs. Gail.

"Mama, can I go over to my friend's house now?"

"Doris Marie, will you give me a chance to get inside and take off my shoes and where are your manners? Say 'Hello' to Mrs. Gail."

"I'm sorry. Hey, Mrs. Gail." I proceeded to give the baby a quick kiss on the forehead.

"Are you taking the baby to the fireworks at Jacksonport this evening?"

"I don't think so Doris Marie. The baby is too small to keep outside too late in the evening. I don't want the mosquitoes to get her."

Gail declined mama's invitation to come inside for ice cream, so mama told her to come by later in the evening and she wasn't taking 'no' for an answer. Mrs. Gail agreed and promised to bring the baby and Glen.

Mama carefully inspected the house and made sure all rooms were cleaned and clothes put away. Even though we hadn't had any company so far today, Mama always liked to be prepared.

Her holiday mantra was "You never know when somebody might decide to drop by."

"You can go for about an hour or so. You need to be back here by five at the least. Don't have Velma and Elliot searching for you all over the neighborhood."

"Yes ma'am, now can we go?" Charlene was quite anxious to get out and chase down some neighborhood fun.

"Y'all can go but Doris Marie, you have to take Larry Wayne with you."

There was a seven year difference between my brother and me. Because of this closeness in age, he often had to tag along with me whenever I left the house.

This was an arrangement that neither of us were particularly thrilled about.

The Backyard Concert

With mama's okay we bolted off on our afternoon quest to make good use of the remaining hours of freedom. The temperature hovered around the high eighties. With the low humidity and a gentle wind blowing, it really wasn't too uncomfortable outside.

The aroma of barbeque and the festive sounds of the holiday echoed throughout the streets. Mr. Carl Kingston had three out of town cars lined up in front of his house. These were his sons-in-law from New Orleans, Chicago, and Dallas. There were two picnic tables set up in his backyard to accommodate all of the Kingston clan.

As I rounded the corner to Garfield Street, I noticed several kids playing 'Red Rover' in front of Mr. Leland Brown's house. Three of the kids belonged to the Brown household and the others were obviously out of town guests. I based this assumption on the license plate of the car parked in front of their house.

"Red Rover, Red Rover, send Gina right over!" With that, the eldest of the Brown children closely examined the linked hands of the opposing team. She targeted the weakest pair of hands and immediately charged full force for the unlucky couple.

"Hey Doris Marie Hey, Larry Wayne." That was Eddie the youngest of the Brown kids and great friends with Larry Wayne.

"Doris Marie, can I go over to Eddie and Melvin's house? Mama won't mind."

"You can visit while I'm at Lillian's. Don't get into trouble and behave yourself."

Larry Wayne joined the group and quickly made friends with the out-of-town guests through Eddie's introductions.

Moments later I arrived at Lillian's house. I went around to the side door and gave a quick knock. I was glad to see that she wasn't outside and I could go in and cool off a bit. It wasn't steamy hot or anything, but the Jarretts had an air conditioner and it would be so relaxing to feel that cool air.

"Is that you Doris Marie?" Mrs. Jarrett was in the den sitting in one of the two big comfy recliners which were positioned right in front of the TV. She had a plate of chicken breast, potato salad, corn on the cob, and baked beans. There was a large glass of iced tea on the end table beside her. Mr. Jarrett was asleep in the matching recliner. He also had a plate, but his had only a few scraps of food left over from what was sure a grand feast.

"Hey, Mrs. Jarrett, Is Lillian home?" It was unusual for Lillian not to be in front of the television.

"Oh, she's up in her room with Emma Jean playing records. You can go on up."

The sound of Smokey Robinson and the Miracles could be heard weaving through the hallway leading to Lillian's room. Both girls were standing in front of Lillian's mirror singing along with the record player.

"Boy, Y'all really stink." Teasing the two was a given. The unwritten kid rule says that I couldn't give an honest assessment of their performance. Because If I was completely honest then I'd have to admit Emma Jean was pretty good.

"Forget you Doris Marie! You're just jealous cause I'm gonna marry Smokey Robinson and sing with him, you know after I kick out all the other Miracles."

I believe that if she could, Lillian WOULD marry Smokey Robinson.

We spent about fifteen more minutes of singing along with Lillian's records. Soon after on Emma Jean's suggestion, we mounted our bikes and decided to explore the goings on throughout the neighborhood.

Before we traveled too far, I had to check on Larry Wayne at the Brown household. Gina assured me that little brother was okay and no trouble. Furthermore, she and her brothers would deliver him safely home before the fireworks activity this evening at Jacksonport.

After checking on Larry Wayne, the girls and I rode down Garfield and saw a few kids playing out in the streets. Their new outfits were *starting to show the wear and tear of the day's play time and heat. I recognized some of them from Larry Wayne's class.*

"Hey, Doris Marie, Hey, Lillian, Hey, Emma Jean!"

"Hey Cassie Hey Dorothy." Only Lillian and I spoke to the girls. Emma Jean continued on as though she didn't hear them.

The sounds of family laughter and the smells of more barbeque floating through the air caused us to make an unexpected detour down Cherry Street. As we rode down the street we found a number of cars in front of Mrs. Peggy Mae Harper's house. She and her husband, Mr. Walter Harper, were playing host to their children who were home for the holiday.

Mrs. Peggy's signature sparkling smile was in full force as she mingled with her backyard guests. We yelled our greetings to the family. A few waved back to us after looking a bit perplexed as to who had spoken to them.

Just as we approached Clay Street we heard a sound which caused us to stop dead in our tracks. It sounded like someone tuning up an electric guitar.

"That's coming from Leonard's house." Emma Jean was the first to note the source of the unusual sound in the neighborhood.

Just as Emma Jean finished speaking, the sound started up again. Only this time, a pleasing melody was coming from the stringed instrument. Just seconds later, another guitar joined in along with what sounded like someone on a keyboard.

Where we being treated to a July Fourth Concert?

"I dare you to go over there, Doris Marie." Lillian offered up a challenge that I gladly took her up on. What she didn't know is that I was going to check it out anyway.......with or without her dare.

The Freeman home was across the street on the corner of Cherry and Clay Street. It was a small white house with a screened in front porch. The yard had been freshly mowed along with the small ditch which separated the house from the street.

I rode my bike around to the back of the house with Emma Jean and Lillian following close behind. To our surprise there were about ten neighborhood kids plus family already in place and ready to listen.

Including the drummer, there were two guitar players with a girl singer. We later learned that the female singer also played the keyboard. Leonard and his cousin were the only people in the band who I knew. The other members of the band were white. This was going to be interesting.

Maybe there was something to that story that Zach and Dexter had told us at the 'free show' last Friday.

"Good afternoon ladies and gentlemen and welcome to our little impromptu concert. My friends and I have been practicing for quite a while and we have put together a few songs we hope you will like. If you will bear with us for just a few more minutes, we will be ready to start."

Leonard addressed the crowd like an old pro. He looked quite professional standing behind the microphone.

"This is so great. I've never been to an actual concert before!" Lillian could hardly contain herself.

"Hey, y'all we have got to go and get Sheritha. She will be so mad at us if we leave her out." I knew that we wouldn't be able to really enjoy the music if we didn't tell our friend.

"Well, y'all can go ahead without me. If you leave now, it will be too crowded when you get back." Our new friend's true colors were showing. Sheritha was our friend. We had known her longer than Emma Jean, so of course we had to get her.

Lillian and I quickly zipped down the street and made it to Sheritha's house in record time. We gave our usual greeting to her family which today included her father, next we pleaded for Sheritha's release. To our surprise, Mrs. Carmen offered up no resistance to us at all.

"We might even walk around there in a few minutes to see the concert for ourselves." Thank God Mrs. Carmen was in an agreeable mood today.

We quickly sped off and arrived back to the Freeman backyard within minutes. However, it wasn't quick enough to regain our original position. I hated to admit it, but Emma Jean was correct. A sizeable crowd had assembled in our absence. This forced us to leave our bikes in the ditch so that we could easily work our way through the crowd. Luckily, we found a place not too far from Emma Jean who was now standing with some of her other buddies.

The band was right in the middle of 'Soul Man' by Sam and Dave. They sounded pretty good too. Oddly enough, the white guy sang lead on this one and not Leonard.

Thunderous shouts of praise for the group were heard throughout the yard:

"They really sound good!"

"Man, they play good enough to be on TV!"

"They should be on American Bandstand!"

The group spent a moment or two to tune up and then started in on their next number. The only girl in the group stepped up to the microphone and started to sing 'Respect' by Aretha Franklin. She gave an amazingly soulful performance of the Atlantic hit. People were looking at each other in total disbelief as this white girl took Aretha's song and made it her very own.

"Folks, that's Miss Penelope Shepherd out of Lincoln, Nebraska."

"She is a looo-oong way from home isn't she?!" Leonard then introduced the other members of the band.

"Next, on drums we have Mr. Calvin Shepherd. Calvin is Penelope's brother. He is also homesick for his mama's home cooking in Lincoln, Nebraska.

The young man playing bass was a local boy from the neighborhood. Actually he was Leonard's first cousin on his Daddy's side. Jerry and Leonard have been playing guitars together since they were little boys. Many people in the crowd were predicting big things for the Freeman boys and their group.

A Kiss For Bobby Joe

The guys had just launched into the Rascal's hit 'Groovin' when I heard my name yelled from somewhere amidst the crowd.

"Hey, Doris Marie!" Oh God! I knew that voice. The torture continues even on the day of our Country's birth. Where are those Minutemen when you need them!

I turned around to find Bobby Joe and two other boys who I didn't know. Two other very cute boys I might add.

"Hey, Bobby Joe, who are your friends?" Bobby Joe gave me a rather curious look. He had an expression on his face which indicated his surprise at my being so nice to him.

"These are my cousins from Saint Louis." Bobby Joe's cousins were two of the handsomest boys I'd ever seen. The older one was a bit taller than his brother and Bobby Joe. He had dark brown hair

which he parted at the right. There was a tiny scar situated in the middle of his forehead which drew attention to his beautiful brown eyes. His name was Spencer and he looked to be about fourteen or fifteen.

His younger brother, Howard, had light reddish brown hair only his parted on the left. Like his older brother, Howard was also quite handsome even if he hadn't quite grown into his ears.

The arrival of the cousins caused Sheritha and Lillian's attention to be momentarily taken away from the music. The band was nearing the end of the Rascal's 'Groovin'. Everyone including Sheritha's parents (who came up soon after we did) was reveling in the soothing music.

The fellas came over and joined us. Bobby Joe on his best behavior introduced them. We tried to engage the guys in conversation but it was difficult with the music being so loud. That was unfortunate because it seemed as though they really enjoyed the band and wanted to talk to us about the music.

The Band gave a spectacular performance but we decided to leave a little before they finished. Bobby Joe and his cousins and the girls and I started to walk toward the Projects. Since the boys weren't on bikes, we pushed ours while walking with them and eventually wound up at the playground.

The neighborhood concert plus the holiday contributed to the virtual barren wasteland which was now the play ground. There were two little kids on the swings and all the other equipment was empty. With no one obstructing our path, we headed straight for the merry-go-round.

"So, Doris Marie, Bobby Joe says that you are his girlfriend." The older boy, Spencer, had a rather devilish grin on his face while asking the question. Why did he have to say that? We were having such a great conversation before this.

"Bobby Joe IS NOT my boyfriend. He really needs to STOP telling everybody that!"

But as soon as I said it, I realized that I had probably embarrassed him. It wasn't so much what I'd just said, but that I'd said it in front of his cousins. And as much as he can be annoying as all get out, he really was a good person and didn't deserve the mean spirited words that had flown out of my mouth.

I had forgotten the number of times Bobby Joe had come to my defense when some of the boys in class teased me.

On more than one occasion, it was Bobby Joe who gave me his cinnamon roll at lunch in addition to saving a seat for me during an assembly.

I shouldn't have been so rough on him especially in front of his cousins.

My sudden outburst had all but silenced our newly formed group. As a result, the merry-go-round was filled with strained conversations and painful looks. Suddenly, I had an idea that would both restore our friends to their earlier happy feelings and give Bobby Joe something to talk about for the rest of the summer.

Without giving it any thought I mustered up the much needed courage and rushed over and planted a BIG KISS right on Bobby Joe's lips! The stunned looks on everyone's face was PRICLESS! That was nothing compared to what happened next. Bobby Joe just turned and slowly started to walk away, but not before uttering the following words:

"I knew you loved me Doris Marie. It was just a matter of time before you could no longer control yourself and jump straight into my arms!!"

Spencer and Howard quickly joined their cousin patted him on the back and called him "The Man". I swear to God they looked like three tanned John Waynes walking off into the sunset.

"So, I guess if you couldn't beat him, you'll join him, right Doris Marie?" Lillian couldn't hold back any longer.

"Naw, I just didn't want Bobby Joe to look bad in front of his cousins." That wasn't a lie. I really didn't want him to look like an idiot in front of his guests.

With all of his grandstanding, boasting and general loudness, Bobby Joe was just a kid who longed to be noticed. For some reason (known only to him) he had zeroed in on me for this needed attention.

Even though he could be 'ten different kinds of worrisome,' Bobby Joe didn't deserve my lashing out at him. This was my way of making it up to him. THANK GOD THE PLAYGROUND WAS EMPTY!

It wasn't long after the boys left that we also decided to leave. We didn't bother to go back to the concert and collect Emma Jean. She seemed to have abandoned us for a more livelier group. I guess we were a little too tame for her.

The day was rapidly drifting into the late afternoon hours and fireworks awaited us at the park in Jacksonport.

Once we deposited Sheritha at her front door, Lillian and I pedaled back to my house for supper and to prepare for the night's activities. We would have to meet Sheritha at the park because she wanted to ride with her father.

"Mama, Lillian is gonna ride with us to the fireworks tonight is that okay?" Lillian was standing directly behind me making it very difficult for Mama to say 'no'.

"Of course she can. Get your mother on the phone so I can get her 'okay."

Lillian quickly summoned her mother on the phone and got the okay. Unknown to the two of us, but not to my mother, was the huge sigh of relief felt by Mrs. Jarret and her husband. Apparently neither of them was up to the challenge of the night's red, white, and blue fireworks' display.

Larry Wayne wound up going with the Brown Family. He had come home before I did with his buddies Melvin and Eddie and Daddy gave his okay.

Counting Velma and Elliot there were five people piling up in Elliot's 1964 Mustang. As always Velma cautioned us about being on our best behavior in his car. Elliot was quite protective of his 'ride.' This meant no food and no muddy shoes!

Jacksonport State Park is a mere three miles from Newport. It is one of many destinations in Northeastern Arkansas for out of town tourists during the summer months. Because the park was located along the White River, the breeze coming off the water would cool things off to make for a comfortable night to enjoy the coming fiery display.

The park was still filling up when we arrived and we were relieved to find out that the fireworks hadn't quite gotten started. This gave us time to explore the park area before things got started.

Daddy had warned us to stay together and not venture too far off from Elliot and Velma.

Adults were milling about looking for the ideal place to set up their lawn chairs. The teenagers were just moving about from one group to another trying to act as though they were too cool to care about something as corny as the Fourth of July fireworks. There were about five car loads of people from Morning Star, First Baptist, and Mt. Moriah Baptist Churches. The parishioners were all carrying mini American flags anxious to show the world their patriotic spirit. A few of the men who were veterans of WWII, wore their army hats and jackets.

We weren't three minutes into our trek when we spotted Zach. He was chatting it up with several kids who appeared to be around his age. One rather tall boy with coal black hair seemed to bear a resemblance to a youthful Clark Kent. There were also two girls in the group both blondes who were giggling at everything the boys were saying.

I recognized another boy from Mr. Sloan's store. I think his name was Jeremy. He like Zach, wore his brown hair in a Beatles' like fashion. The few times I saw him in the store his head was buried deep in a MAD magazine.

We were almost past the group when from the corner of my eye, I saw Zach approaching us.

"Hey, Lillian and Doris Marie! Hey Charlene! I didn't know that I would see you guys here this evening. Where's your little brother?"

Lillian spoke up and gave out the information about Larry Wayne. I must say that I was surprised to see her speak to Zach in such a friendly manner. Her earlier behavior demonstrated that he was not a favorite of hers. Maybe she was trying to see him in a different light as I had with Bobby Joe.

"Uh, Zach who are your friends?" Of course that question came from Charlene a person whose curiosity is exceeded only by her boldness.

"Those were just some kids from school, except that short blonde hair girl. That's my Cousin Rita from Blytheville."

As if on cue, the group turned and gave a friendly wave in our direction. After a few moments of polite conversation, we walked Zach back over to the others as we continued on our exploration.

"Hey, Big Head!" It was Larry Wayne and his buddies. They were running around like little fellas will do once you set them free on the general public.

"Hey, Larry Wayne you having a good time?" Of course he's having a good time. He can hardly stand still long enough to say the few words he had uttered.

"Yeah, and guess what?! We are going to pop some more firecrackers when we get home.

Oh God! I hope he meant at his friends' house. I am in no mood for MORE firecrackers this evening

I didn't have time to respond because he and his buddies ran off to find more adventures.

The fireworks were spectacular! The sun had finally gone down and the dark summer sky served as a canvas for the emerging fiery colors. All we heard from the crowd was a myriad of 'oohs' and 'ahs' and 'look at that!'

After about forty minutes the evening's festivities were about to come to an end. To avoid the rush of cars leaving the park, Elliot gathered up everyone to abandon the park.

Sheritha's Date With Her Father

When we got home we found mama and Daddy saying goodnight to Glen and his 'little family.' Mama had kept Gail to her earlier promise of coming over later for a visit. This new phrase of 'little family' is how mama now referred to Glen and Gail with the new baby.

We got some chips and a soda from the kitchen and set out for our bedroom. On the way, Lillian grabbed Velma's record player and a few of her records.

We put on the Miracles' latest album 'Going to A Go-Go' and proceeded to sing the title track. The girls and I stood in front of the mirror of the old dresser which stood in the far corner of our bedroom. We practiced our dance steps while singing along with the record. We could all dance the 'Jerk' and the 'Monkey' pretty good and seeing ourselves dancing helped out a lot. After a while we ventured away from the comfort zone of the dresser's mirror to other parts of the bedroom still keeping in time with music.

We were in the middle of "The Tracks of my Tears" when mama called me to the phone.

It was Sheritha who earlier had opted out of going to Jacksonport. "Y'all going to the social at the gym? It starts at 7:30."

"I'll ask Mama, she'll probably say yes since you're going." My mother knew and admired how strict Sheritha's folks were on her. If they were okay with her going to the dance it would most likely be okay with my folks too.

I ran back to my room to share the news with the girls. We decided to approach mama and daddy as a united front. We made sure that Lillian went with us to give us an edge. Daddy might find it hard to say no if we presented an extra set of sad eyes.

Mama and daddy were in the kitchen seated at the table talking. Mama had her usual cup of coffee while daddy nursed a glass of buttermilk. Daddy was relating the evening's events with mama. He was telling her about the conversation he had with Glen.

"Willie, I hope you didn't scare the boy too much. This is his first child and he and Gail won't want any more if you scare him to death!" I don't know what Daddy had said to frighten the new father, but the way mama was smiling while she lightly chastised him suggested it wasn't too serious.

It was Daddy who first noticed the three of us standing in the kitchen hall way. Still in a good mood, he immediately got up from the table and started to do the Temptation Walk while singing MY GIRL.

Of course Lillian found this to be hilarious. After seeing her reaction, mama got up to perform along with daddy. Her singing was a little better than daddy, but not her dancing. When it came to dancing mama was somewhat limited in her steps. She seemed to favor moving only her left foot back and forth. It looked as though it took a considerable amount of thought to move her right foot or to occasionally clap her hands!

"Mama, you and daddy need to quit! Y'all know you can't dance!" I wasn't too surprised by mama getting up and dancing, but this was a rare treat on my father's part. He rarely showed this 'fun' side of himself. Butterbean was usually quite conservative in his everyday life.

"Uh, Mama can we go to the social at the gym tonight? That's what Sheritha was telling me on the phone. Before you say no remember

that Lillian and I will be in eighth grade this year and Charlene will be in the ninth. We're old enough to go down the street to the gym"

With that last statement, we tried to look very serious. . . . and sad.

Before mama or daddy had a chance to speak, Charlene decided to add her two cents. "Velma and Elliot will be there too. So, can we go please?"

"Okay, you can go but you have to be back home at nine. Lillian, I will call your parents for you." It seemed that daddy was relieved to stop dancing to answer our question. I think he was also a little winded.

"Wait a minute, Willie. Who's going to be there to chaperone this dance?" In the excitement, daddy was about to release us without knowing about our protectors. During the school year it would have been the high school teachers, but he hadn't thought about who would be there during this summer dance.

"I know who will be there Mrs. Gurthalean. My mother said that some of the teachers volunteered. Also the Ladies Auxillary and a few of the Deacons from Shady Grove Baptist Church are going to be there to chaperone.

Mama told us to go ahead and freshen up a bit while she made a phone call to the Jarrets to confirm Lillian's information.

It didn't take us long to ready ourselves for the night's dance. There was excitement in the air at the anticipation of going to a social and staying out until late. A quick washing up in the bathroom helped us to freshen up from the day's activities. Fortunately, the heat of the day hadn't wilted the curls we'd just gotten on last Saturday.

We were looking forward to seeing a number of our classmates plus high school kids would be there too. It was certain that we were going to have a good time even if we did have a curfew of nine o'clock.

Mama took another call from Sheritha who said that she and her father would be by later to take us to the dance. Mama gave her 'okay' and said that we'd be ready and waiting for them when they came.

To get into the mood of the evening and calm our nerves, we decided to listen to some more of Velma's records. Luckily, she was off with Elliot and couldn't fuss at us for using her things.

Charlene put on the Supreme's 'Love Is Here and Now You're Gone.'

Hair brushes and a ruler were used as microphones. As usual we consented to Lillian to be Diana Ross. She may be asked to relinquish this role when Sheritha gets here.

I must admit that Lillian could do a pretty good job of mimicking Diana. She had the moves and facial expressions down pat.

Sheritha and her father, Mr. Pete, arrived about twenty minutes later. Not only was he chauffeuring us to the dance, but he was going to stay as his daughter's date. My mother told Mr. Pete that this was very sweet of him to do this for his daughter. She then hugged Sheritha and told her that this was going to be a very special evening for both her and her father.

Before leaving for the social, Mr. Pete spent a few more minutes getting caught up with mama and daddy. My parents had known Mr. Pete for some time. He had grown up around the Augusta area and was good friends with daddy's brother, Uncle BJ.

Upon our arrival to the gym, we could hear Marvin Gaye and Tammi Terrell's 'Ain't No Mountain High Enough' being played.

Dexter White and Lynn Smalls were settled on the stage with two microphones carefully placed on either side of the two large record players.

Lynn would play livelier tunes that got EVERYONE on the floor. Dexter played the slower tunes which gave the older kids an excuse to dance close together.

The gym was decorated with about three hundred red, white, and blue balloons. There were similarly colored streamers along the walls in front of the bleachers, and lined along the bottom of the stage.

There were also several tables set up with sodas and popcorn. The Shady Grove Youth Group had a table filled with bags of chips and jars of pickles. These items were priced at ten and fifteen cents respectively. They were hoping to make a nice little profit that evening and use the proceeds to go toward their trip to an amusement park in Memphis.

We hadn't been there very long when Mr. Pete spotted some old friends of his. He excused himself assuring us that he would be right back shortly after his visit.

We began to stir about the area to see who was there. After a while, we ran up on the 'Cheryls' who were classmates of Charlene. They were two best friends with the same first name. One was Cheryl

Lamb and the other was Cheryl Patterson. The two were standing alongside the back wall talking and eyeing all the young men in the gym.

We left Charlene with her friends and continued on our stroll around the gym. We stopped at one of the stands and bought popcorn and sodas.

We were enjoying our snacks when we noticed some of the adults had ventured onto the dance floor. This caused us to laugh especially hard when Lillian told Sheritha about Mama and daddy's dance-off earlier in the evening.

Suddenly Lynn put The Bar Kays' latest on the record player. "Soul Finger" was a great tune that got everyone dancing and singing along with the record.

"SOUL FINGER!"

"SOUL FINGER!"

"SOUL FINGER!"

"YEAH!!!!!!!!!!!!"

We raced onto the dance floor along with everyone else. Dancing the 'Swim' and the 'Jerk' in front of the mirror at home was paying off. If I do say so myself, I could hold my own with the other kids moving around on the dance floor.

"Hey, Baby Girl! Mind if I cut in?" Sheritha's father appeared and took her by the hand and proceeded to twirl her around and around.

There was a look of total contentment on Sheritha's face. You could tell that she was totally devoted to her father.

Mr. Pete could move pretty well for someone's parent. He was certainly better than my father, but that wasn't hard to beat. Although, I wasn't at all certain of it, I think that Mr. Pete was doing the 'Jerk.'

Sheritha didn't look the least bit embarrassed even though Mr. Pete did look a little comical on the dance floor.

It was now time for Dexter to play a record. If he kept to the apparent system that he and Lynn had agreed to, then this should be a slow song.

"People say I'm the life of the party 'cause I tell a joke or two."

After the music started, Lillian and I started to walk off the dance floor. Sheritha had turned and was about to join us, when her father grabbed her hand and asked for another dance.

I didn't think that our friend could look any happier than she had earlier this evening, but now she was literally beaming! Tonight she had her father all to herself and she was on 'cloud nine.'

"She looks happy doesn't she, Doris Marie?" Lillian was smiling almost as hard as Sheritha. This is the kind of sentimental stuff that she loved.

I was about to agree with her when the 'thorn in my side' once again appeared.

"Hey Doris Marie. I'm here and you don't have to be worried anymore about finding a dance partner!"

It's Bobby Joe and his cousin Spencer. I guess Howard decided to sit out tonight's social.

I had a gnawing suspicion that Bobby Joe would show up tonight, it was just a matter of time. Hopefully, he won't be so obnoxious with his cousin along with him.

Remembering the harsh words I'd used earlier on the playground made me rethink my approach to Bobby Joe. I then decided to take the high road and treat him with lots of respect, maybe he will reciprocate and act like a civilized human being.

"Hey Bobby Joe, I was hoping to see you this evening." The shocked looks on the faces of my friends and his cousin were priceless. Lillian's mouth was actually partially open in sort of a gasp.

The least shocked was Bobby Joe who must have still been thinking about the 'kiss' I gave him earlier this evening. My guess is he was probably hoping for another kiss only this time he would be prepared.

"Who's that young man?" Mr. Pete seemed to be mildly amused by the whole thing. Sheritha had stopped dancing and turned around to witness the exchange.

What happened next even took me by surprise. I asked Bobby Joe to dance with me! This was my way of taking the initiative and beating Bobby Joe at his own game. He couldn't loud talk me in to a dance if I asked him first!

A low range "okay" was all that Bobby Joe could muster up. He looks a little bewildered but he goes along with my request anyway.

I pulled him onto the dance floor which was no easy task considering how sweaty his hands were.

Spencer gathered up Lillian and the two of them joined us for the last part of the Smokey Robinson tune.

"This afternoon you kissed me and now we're dancing. I thought you hated me, Doris Marie."

"Well, Bobby Joe, I don't now nor have I ever hated you. But you do annoy me. As a matter of fact you seem to go out of your way to annoy me!"

After relating this fact Bobby Joe insisted that I tell him just HOW he annoyed me.

"How? You scream my name out every time you see me! You keep telling people you love me and that we are going to get married! You are always and forever making those stupid kissing faces! That would be the annoying part!"

These revelations only seem to make Bobby Joe's chest pump up twice its size. That big goofy grin on his face got even bigger showing even more teeth!

"Oh Girl, I knew you'd come around. Nobody can resist these 'Smokey Robinson' good looks."

"Yeah, you look like Smokey alright. . . Smokey the Bear!!"

Bobby Joe and his cousin kept Lillian and me on the dance floor all evening. When he wasn't being annoying, Bobby Joe could actually be a lot of fun.

It was about eight thirty and Lynn had just put on James Brown's 'Cold Sweat.' Everyone jumped onto the dance floor. This time Mr. Pete stood back and insisted that Sheritha dance with her friends.

Bobby Joe got so into the record that he did the 'James Brown' split!

It would have been great too if Spencer didn't have to help him up from the floor.

Just when I thought the evening couldn't get any more special, something very sweet happened. I danced a slow dance with Bobby Joe.

Both Lillian and I had managed to avoid dancing the slow songs all evening. We'd excuse ourselves to the bathroom or go to the snack bar. Sometimes we'd just make sure we'd engage them in conversation. But this time we'd have to face the music. Besides, this was a great song. 'Hey Love' by Stevie Wonder was one of our favorites.

The music started and the fellas led us to the dance floor. I was a little nervous because I'd never danced a slow dance with a boy before. Fortunately, I had been watching the older kids all evening and I think I had the hang of it. Lillian looked completely confident.

Bobby Joe was a good dancer and it was easy to follow his lead. I really enjoyed it. There was only one moment of concern when it seemed Bobby Joe tried to pull me closer. I resisted and he didn't try it again. Honestly, I think he was relieved that I pushed him away!

Mr. Willie, I Brought Your Daughter Home!

That would indeed be the last dance for us. After this song we had to say our goodbyes to Sheritha and her father then collect Charlene and start for home.

Mr. Pete offered to drive us back, but Bobby Joe and his cousin convinced him to let them walk us home. Sheritha's father agreed but with a condition.

Spencer and Bobby Joe could walk us back to our house, but Sheritha and her dad would follow close behind in his car!

Needless to say that was a strange walk back to the house. At least it was for me. Not so much for Bobby Joe and Spencer, they talked the whole time. They didn't mind having Mr. Pete's car just a few feet behind us. I still found it a bit odd, especially when I was certain that I heard Mr. Pete laugh a few times!

When we get to the house, we see that Daddy had the front porch light on. We stood and talked to the fellas for a few more minutes. Unfortunately, the mosquitoes started to make their appearance and we had to cut our visit short.

Charlene and Lillian said their 'goodbyes' and quickly went inside. Spencer stepped toward the front sidewalk leaving Bobby Joe and me to end our evening.

"Admit it you had a good time tonight didn't ya' Doris Marie?"

"I had a very good time, Bobby Joe, but I better go in now before my Daddy comes out here."

"Okay, Okay, uh you taking French this year?" Poor Bobby Joe, being civilized was not going to be easy for him.

"They don't offer French at Branch... do they?" I wasn't kidding I really did want to know.

"I heard that they were getting another teacher this year and French would be offered."

Well, if he was lying, he was very convincing.

"Yea, Bobby Joe, like you are going to take French."

"If you take the class, then I'll take the class." Bobby Joe made his point by gently poking my forehead.

Okay it's official I do like this new and improved Bobby Joe... that's if he's for real.

"Doris Marie, say good night to your friend and come inside."

Thank God it was mama and not Daddy calling from inside the house. I had better go on in, because the next time she'd be outside to escort me into the house.

"I gotta go. It's getting late. Maybe I'll see you at the playground tomorrow." Oh God, did I just say that? EW!

"About what time will you be there?" Bobby Joe was really serious about this meeting tomorrow.

I told him that the girls and I could be there at around three-thirty. He agreed and said that he and the cousins would be there on time.

And then IT happened, another strange occurrence. Bobby Joe kissed me... on the lips!

Okay, so it wasn't a Hollywood kiss like in the movies. It happened very quickly and both of us had our eyes opened!

But I must say that I LIKED IT!

A split second later it was over and Bobby Joe and his cousin quickly got into Mr. Pete's car. On Sheritha's insistence he had hung around to give the boys a ride to Second Street where Bobby Joe lived.

When I turned around to go up the steps to the house, Mama was waiting for me at the door. She had a slight smile on her face, but didn't say anything. She just gave me a warm hug and then she went to bed.

I went to the kitchen where Charlene and Lillian were seated and eating chocolate ice cream. They even had the radio on that station out of Nashville. It played a little too much 'blues' for us, but they did get some Motown in the mix.

"You want some ice cream?" Lillian was simultaneously offering up the creamy delight and getting the bowl and spoon.

"Honestly, I'm a little stuffed from all the junk we had at the social, but I guess I'll take a little."

The two were surprisingly quiet. So far nobody has asked me about Bobby Joe. I know they want to because there's a silly grin on both of their faces.

"Doris Marie." Alright, here it comes. I knew Charlene wouldn't be able to hold it in. My defenses are up and I'm ready for it.

"Did you see Sheritha's father doing the 'Jerk?'"

Really? This was her question?

Just then Lillian chimed in with her two cents. "He wasn't that bad. I thought they looked cute together."

Maybe they weren't going to tease me to death about this evening. It was getting late and we would soon have to go to bed. Maybe they were going to postpone the teasing for tomorrow. I MADE IT!!

Or so I thought I had. Apparently, I didn't see my father hiding in the hallway by the bathroom.

"MR. WILLIE, I BROUGHT YOUR DAUGHTER HOME!!"

Oh God! It was Daddy. I thought he was asleep. I'll bet he was listening at the window the whole time while Bobby Joe was here!

Now the long awaited laughter and teasing begins.

"Doris Marie and Bobby Joe sitting in a tree. . . . ."

Even Larry Wayne joins in and I could have sworn I saw him fast asleep when I passed by his bed just moments ago.

"Alright, Alright! That's enough of the teasing. Leave my baby alone now"

As usual, mama was here to save me.

"I'm sorry Baby Girl. I guess it's okay if you want to have a little friend. . . no boyfriend just a friend. You're too young to be keeping company.

Now, I had to laugh. . . but to myself. I had to admit that it was cute the way my father was teasing me and reminding me to be 'a good girl' all at the same time.

The teasing didn't last for too long. As a matter of fact, the conversation soon turned to all of the great records that the guys were spinning tonight. Of course we had to comment on how cute Dexter looked. We were also a little saddened to see that he had a date with him tonight. I recognized her from the wedding. She was the young lady with the basketball size afro.

Mama cautioned us about staying up too late and ordered us to make sure we were in bed by ten o'clock. So, one by one we bathed and went to bed.

When Lillian spent the night, I had to double up with Charlene in her bed letting our company use mine. We did this because Lillian was an only child and was used to her own space.

With mama's approval, we took the kitchen radio to our room on the promise that we wouldn't turn it up too loud. We continued to listen to the Nashville station hoping that they would play more Motown and Memphis hits.

"Doris Marie, do you really like Bobby Joe?" Lillian's question didn't have the air of playfulness, but was quite serious.

"He's alright." I asked her if she'd noticed how mature he was acting tonight.

"You know, he could have been his usual nutsy, loud self. . . especially when he was standing outside the house."

"Mr. Willie was waiting on Bobby Joe to scream out that he had brought you home!"

"You know, Lillian, if his cousins are still here on Friday, maybe we can all go to the free show at the Strand."

I did have a good time tonight and I wanted to continue it. Hopefully, Bobby Joe was maturing and this wasn't just a show he was putting on for his out of town guests.

We talked for another half hour or so before drifting off to sleep. With all the activity of the day, we had a very restful night.

Fortunately, the next day was Wednesday, Mama's day off. She probably wouldn't bug us about staying in bed for too long. We'd had a very active and adventurous Holiday, we could use a few extra hours of sleep.

Chapter 10

Growing up, It's Not So Bad! Wednesday, July, 5

I got up before Charlene or Lillian. One reason was the aroma of mama's coffee which saturated every room of the house. The other reason was Charlene had completely taken over the bed. She had me wedged against the wall as she always did whenever we had to sleep together.

When I found my way to the kitchen after washing up, I saw Mama sitting at the table with Velma. They were deep in conversation while sipping their steaming cups of coffee.

Thank God Daddy had left for work quite a while ago. I wouldn't have to hear him tease me about my Bobby Joe encounter from last night.

I could see Gurt's famous biscuit bread on the stove. There was a platter of scrambled eggs and another filled with sausages. The abundance of food was proof positive that our little brother had yet to make his presence known at the breakfast table.

"Well Hello Miss Lady. I heard you had a very interesting night."

This was a little peculiar. My oldest sister was joking with me like I was one of her girlfriends.

"The social was lots of fun. You should have seen Sheritha dancing with her father. But where were you? I thought you and Elliot were going to the social"

"Uh, excuse you. We came much later. We were over to Laura's house, not that it's any of YOUR business, Miss 'I just GOT a boyfriend!'"

I had forgotten that Velma wasn't here last night when I got in from the dance and my unofficial date with Bobby Joe. Not only was she teasing me but she had the nerve to make a little joke too.

"Leave your little sister alone, Velma. Bobby Joe is a nice young fella. . . . a little loud, but still a good kid."

Mama gave me a quick wink. Again this was Gurt's way of showing her support for me.

Later in the day Charlene accompanied Lillian and me to meet with Bobby Joe and his cousins at the playground. We first decided to stop by Sheritha's house to see if we could convince her to go along with us.

We knew that Sheritha was still visiting with her father. We were surprised to learn that she was making plans to go back to Chicago with him on the following day.

Mr. Pete had a new wife and he wanted his daughter to get to know her. We could tell that Sheritha was excited about going and we were happy for her. But there was a little sadness among us all, because we were going to seriously miss our buddy. Fortunately, Miss Sheritha was scheduled to return in a month.

"You sure you don't want to go with us to the playground? You won't have to stay long."

I asked even though I was quite aware of the answer. Even though she was heading out with her father tomorrow, Sheretha would shadow him until they actually left. It was as though she was frightened that he would leave without her, which of course he wouldn't.

We did visit for a while and then said our goodbyes and promised to keep her up to date on Bobby Joe and his cousins.

We left our friend's house and made a mad dash to the playground. Surprisingly, there wasn't that many people on the equipment. The twins, Jason and Janet Allen, were on the swings trying to see who could go higher. They lived here in Calhoun Circle. It has only been lately that their parents have let them come to the playground without older brother Clayton following close behind them.

There were several teenage boys going way too fast on the merry-go-round. Undoubtedly, they were trying to see who would be the first to go flying off into the surrounding dirt.

Mrs. Carmen had given us some frozen lemonade cups to take with us. The cold lemony delights served as a great coolant as we perched ourselves at the very top of the monkey bars.

We weren't there for long before the boys showed up on their bikes.

"Hello, ladies." This greeting came from Spencer. "Where did y'all get those sip dips?"

"We've been over to Sheritha's house and her mama gave them to us."

Just as I was answering the cousin, Bobby Joe climbed up the bars and squeezed in between Lillian and me. Spencer followed him and sat beside Charlene, while Howard the younger cousin sat directly beneath us.

Later after about twenty minutes when the heat of the day got to be a little too much, we sought refuge under a neighboring tree.

The cousins proved to be a very lively bunch and they really brought out the best in Bobby Joe.

The two were in honors programs at their school and participated in different activities sponsored by their local Boy's Club.

One time there was a talent show at the Boy's Club and the cousins and a few of their friends did a Temptations' song. Spencer and Howard got up and demonstrated their routine for us. They did a very good job imitating the famous "Temp' steps and spins while singing 'My Girl'.

We stayed at the playground for about forty more minutes and then we had to head for home. The boys rode their bikes with us to Mason Street for Lillian and on to Clay Street for Charlene and me. I was really happy to see that neither mama nor daddy was in our yard when we got there. Daddy would have had a million questions for the boys.

Sheritha called later that evening. She was genuinely interested in hearing about Bobby Joe's cousins. I told her all about them and how much fun we'd had on the playground.

We talked for a few more minutes in which time she shared with me her father's phone number and address in Chicago. We promised to keep in contact while she was away.

We did go to the free show at the Strand on Friday with the guys.

'Beach Blanket Bingo' was playing. Even though we thought it was pretty corny, parts of the movie had us laughing out loud. We especially liked the Eric Von Zipper character.

Spencer, Howard, and Bobby Joe became regular fixtures at our house and at Lillian's as well. In addition to our visits on the playground, the fellas also accompanied us to Vacation Bible School at Morning Star. We even got them interested in listening to the Beatles and reading Mad Magazine.

Bobby Joe and I spent a considerable amount of time together during that summer.

We rode our bikes all around town together. We paid regular visits to Sloan's Grocery for candy and to Ryans' Drugstore for MAD Magazines and other comics.

Lillian would sometimes accompany us on these outings. She and Emma Jean were still friends and would remain so for years to come. Oddly enough Emma Jean started to 'rub off' on me.

Lillian must have been a good influence on her because she had lost all of her 'bullying' ways!

Lillian and I were still close even if we didn't hang out quite as much as we use to. Even though our sleepovers were becoming less and less, we did try to make sure we talked regularly on the phone. One day Mrs. Jarrett even let us call Sheritha in Chicago.

Our buddy returned as promised in the first week of August. She was sporting an 'afro' which made her look like a real teenager.

Then again maybe it wasn't the afro, maybe it was just her new look on life.

Sheritha did seem to be spending a lot of time talking more about issues concerning the world like the war in Vietnam and Civil Rights.

Lillian was afraid that maybe Sheritha had outgrown us and I must say that I had my concerns also. Mama told us not to worry and that Sheritha's new experiences in Chicago introduced her to new and different people. Her new demeanor was just a reflection of those new experiences.

Our friend didn't abandon us altogether. Sheritha did occasionally accompany us to the Friday Free Show. It was rare for her to ride bikes with us or go to Sloan's grocery for treats. Oddly enough, she started to hang out more with Charlene and her friends.

Every kid (and teachers too) knows that as soon as the Fourth of July Holiday is over, summer comes to a rapid close. And so it was with the Summer of 1967.

Velma left for college the last week of August. Daddy and mama packed the basic essentials into his car and made the drive to Pine Bluff. Because of the limited space, Charlene and I said our goodbyes and stayed at home so that Larry Wayne could go. Velma and Elliot would come back later on to get her remaining items.

The first day of school was September fifth. We wore our traditional 'first day of school' new outfits and tried not to sweat out our newly pressed hair. I had gone with my 'That Girl' look of full bangs and a flip.

The weather was still hot, so sleeveless dresses and shorts sets were the order of the day.

And wouldn't you know it? Bobby Joe was right about the new French class being offered. But it wasn't for eighth graders. We'd have to wait another year before we could take the class.

This would be the first year that my sister's friends wouldn't be stopping by to walk with us to school. But a new tradition was born this September because Bobby Joe came by to walk with Charlene, Larry Wayne and me.

These walks with Bobby Joe would continue throughout the year and onto high school.

My brother Charles Landrum circa 1960

My brother Jerry Landrum circa 1969

My sister Velma Landrum-White circa 1967

My Mother Gurtha Landrum circa 1953

My father Willie Landrum circa 1950

My sister Velma Landrum-White circa 1950

My brother Charles Landrum circa 1950

Epilogue

I grew up in a small southern town in northeastern Arkansas during one of the most significant times in American history. The church bombings, riots, sit-ins and worst of all the assassinations happened with such frequency, that it almost became the norm to see it played out on TV. It got to the point that you literally held your breath whenever a news bulletin flashed across the screen.

A harsh reality of life is learning that the world can be a very unkind place. But you also learn that life goes on and you have to find joy whenever you can. I wasn't defined by the events being played out across the country. This is not to say that I wasn't affected by it either.

Directly or indirectly the world did find its way into my life and our small town.

Including my brother, many young men from Newport and surrounding counties fought in Viet Nam. Sadly, North East Arkansas also suffered many casualties from this terrible war.

Through the blessing of television, we watched the historic March on Washington and witnessed the heinous acts committed against young Civil Rights workers. It was truly inspirational to see black people speaking out about injustices all over the country.

I believe this energized the young people of our town to seek higher education to help make a difference in the world.

I will end my story in the same fashion as I began. . . . my wonderment of the summer of 1967 in the small town of Newport, Arkansas.

67' was the year that I truly discovered boys and got my first kiss. I had an enormous crush on Smokey Robinson and I desperately wanted to marry my 7ᵗʰ grade science teacher, Mr. Long.

This was the year that the bond between my friends and I grew stronger while we simultaneously started on our own individual paths.

In the summer of 1967 I was just a kid doing what kids do. I rode my bike and visited with friends and family in my neighborhood.

When I wasn't watching my favorite TV shows, I was listening to all the different groups on the radio. I didn't realize it then, but I was tuned in to music that would later serve as the narration to the social landscape of the time.

They say it takes a village to raise a child. Our village was filled with the World War Two and Depression Era generation. They were people who knew hard times up close and personal. Many came from farms and cotton fields and all worked to make a better life for their children.

Every time I have a conversation with anyone who is near my age or older certain inevitable questions always arise like:

"How did they (our parents) manage to keep a roof over our heads?"

OR

"How did mama and daddy feed all of us?"

We always speak in glowing terms of our parents' continuous efforts to maintain a stable household. Through their hard work, they demonstrated courage, strength, pride and a determination to make a better life for their children.

Was it a perfect childhood? No, it wasn't Mayberry by any stretch of the imagination. But I can say that some of my most cherished memories are of growing up at 305 Clay Street especially during the summer of 1967.

The End

Printed in the United States
By Bookmasters